GEORGE S.
PATTON

Illustrated by Meryl Henderson

GEORGE S. PATTON
War Hero

by George E. Stanley

ALADDIN PAPERBACKS

New York   London   Toronto   Sydney

❧

ALADDIN PAPERBACKS
An imprint of Simon & Schuster Children's Publishing Division
1230 Avenue of the Americas, New York, NY 10020
Text copyright © 2007 by George E. Stanley
Illustrations copyright © 2007 by Meryl Henderson
All rights reserved, including the right of reproduction
in whole or in part in any form.
ALADDIN PAPERBACKS and related logo are
registered trademarks of Simon & Schuster, Inc.
CHILDHOOD OF FAMOUS AMERICANS is a
registered trademark of Simon & Schuster, Inc.
Designed by Lisa Vega
The text of this book was set in New Caledonia.
Manufactured in the United States of America
First Aladdin Paperbacks edition October 2007
4 6 8 10 9 7 5 3
Library of Congress Control Number 2006937133
ISBN-13: 978-1-4169-1547-8
0423 SKY

ILLUSTRATIONS

CONTENTS

GEORGE S.
PATTON

The Pattons of Virginia

"Good Lord, no!" Susan Patton cried.

At the sound of his mother's voice, eight-year-old George William rushed to the parlor door. Susan was clutching a Union newspaper in her right hand, and tears were streaming down her face.

"Mama! What's wrong?"

"Your father's dead!" Susan said. She choked back a sob and let the newspaper fall to the floor.

George William picked it up and scanned the front page. At the bottom, he saw his father's name. Colonel George Smith Patton had died near Winchester, Virginia, after the Confederate troops he commanded were overrun by Union soldiers.

When George William looked at his mother again, though, the tears were gone, replaced by a look of determination. "Help me get everything ready, son," she said. "We must bring your father back home to be buried."

The next morning, Susan headed to Winchester. She was accompanied by George William; the three younger children, Nellie, Glassell, and Susie; and her personal servant, Peter.

In 1864 the state of Virginia was a devastated land because of the American Civil War. Fields had been laid waste, once-grand mansions were in ruins, and, just like George Smith Patton, thousands of other men and boys had died in battle.

When the family arrived to claim Colonel Patton's body, they were told that he had already been buried, but the officer in charge gave Susan her husband's horse, saddle, and sword.

The war finally ended in April 1865, but the outlook for Susan Patton and her children was bleak. She worried constantly about how they were going to survive. Her prayers were soon answered when she received a letter, along with $600, from her brother Andrew Glassell, a lawyer living in Southern California. He wanted them to come west. Susan accepted his offer, and the family arrived in California on December 19, 1866.

Although Susan thought California seemed strange after having lived all of her life in Virginia, George William, who was ten years old, liked the sunny climate. And as the man of the family, he took on the responsibility of caring for his mother and his brother and sisters. Soon, though, George William began to miss Virginia, and he longed to go back there,

but he knew that he was remembering the good times when his father was alive and not the Virginia that had been ravaged by war.

Susan had given George William his father's sword and saddle, and he treasured these keepsakes. One day in 1868 he decided he needed to do something to honor his father's memory, so, with his family's blessing, he changed his name from George William Patton to George Smith Patton II.

That same year, Colonel Patton's friend and former classmate at Virginia Military Institute (VMI), George H. Smith, arrived in California to start a new life. He began to practice law with George's uncle Andrew. He also began to spend more time with George's family and, in 1870, he asked Mrs. Patton to marry him. She accepted, and her son was absolutely delighted. In the evenings, after dinner, George would sit next to his stepfather and listen to stories about Colonel Patton's bravery and heroism in battle. At times, George would close his eyes and pretend that it was his own father who was telling him these things.

At school, George was a good student. He worked hard and he made the honor roll regularly, but the stories about his father only made him miss Virginia more, and he still longed to return there. In 1874 George got his wish when he entered Virginia Military Institute.

After graduation in 1877 George remained at VMI for another year as a professor of French, but he missed his family and he knew his mother was dying of cancer. In 1878 George returned to Los Angeles to study law. He passed the California bar exam in 1880.

One evening, George entered his mother's bedroom, pulled up a chair and, taking her hand in his, said, "How are you feeling?"

His mother sighed. "About the same, George, about the same," she said. "What is it that you want to tell me?"

George smiled. "I could never keep anything from you, could I, Mother?" he said.

"No, you couldn't, and why would you want to?" his mother said. "Is it about a young lady?"

Now George laughed. "You're incorrigible, Mother," he said, "but that's one of the things I've always loved about you."

"Oh, mothers always know when their sons are in love, George," his mother said. "Tell me about her."

"She's Ruth Wilson," George said. "Her father was Benjamin Davis Wilson."

"Ah, Don Benito," his mother said. "An amazing man, from the stories I've heard about him."

"They're all true, Mother," George said. "My only regret is that I never met him."

Benjamin Davis Wilson was famous throughout the area for the adventurous life he had led before settling down and becoming the head of one of Southern California's leading families. He died in 1878, at the age of sixty-seven.

Not long after the conversation with his mother, George proposed to Ruth, and they were married on December 11, 1884. It was one of the season's most important social events. George and Ruth moved into the Wilson estate, a large, ranch-style house called Lake Vineyard, located in what would become the southwestern corner of the city of Pasadena. The house had been the pride and joy of Ruth's father. It sat on 1,300 acres of land and was covered with thousands of grape vines; orange, lemon, and lime trees; and several hundred olive and walnut trees.

Two months after they were married, George and Ruth learned that they were going to have a child. More than anything else in the world, George wanted a son. He got his wish on November 11, 1885, when George Smith

Patton, Jr., was born. The family decided to call him Georgie.

One morning, George went into the bedroom where Ruth was nursing Georgie and said, "You've made me so happy, dear. You've given me a beautiful son. No man could ask for anything more than that."

When Ruth turned her head away from him, George gently took her chin and pulled it back.

"Ruth, you're crying," George said. "What's the matter?"

"I'm worried about the baby," Ruth said. "I think there's something wrong with him."

"You're just tired, sweetheart," George assured her. "He looks perfectly healthy to me."

"No, George, I'm not just tired," Ruth said. "I think you should get the doctor."

George stood up. "All right, if that will make you feel better, dear," he said.

Dr. Meshew arrived within the hour, examined Georgie, told Ruth that he was sure everything would be all right, but privately told George that he was worried about the boy.

"What do you mean?" George demanded. "What's wrong with him?"

"It's difficult to tell, Mr. Patton," Dr. Meshew said. "Some babies just aren't very strong when they're born."

"I don't want to hear this, Dr. Meshew," George said angrily. "I expect you to do whatever is necessary to ensure that my son survives."

Dr. Meshew took a deep breath and let it out. "Please understand me, Mr. Patton, that I try to make sure all of my patients remain healthy."

"I'm sorry, Dr. Meshew, it's just that . . ." George stopped, unable to continue.

Dr. Meshew put his hand on George's shoulder. "You don't need to apologize, sir," he said. "My wife and I lost our first child, and I've yet to get over it, so there is no way I would want you to go through the same thing."

10

Just then, Mary Scally walked up to the two men. She was a devout Irish-Catholic woman who had been hired as Georgie's nurse.

"I am sorry to interrupt you, gentlemen, but I'm worried that Mrs. Patton is tiring herself out trying to get sweet Georgie to nurse," she said, "so if I could just take the precious boy from her, I think I can get him to take milk from my finger again."

George had seen Mary perform this miracle before—dipping her finger in a glass of milk, then putting it in Georgie's mouth. He thought that might be a good idea, even though he knew it upset Ruth, who thought she was a failure as a mother.

"Thank you, Mary," George said. "Mrs. Patton is very tired, so please tell her that I said she needs her rest."

Mary entered the bedroom and within minutes had reappeared with Georgie in her arms.

George watched as Mary started down the

stairs, his son cradled against her shoulder.

"I think she loves that child almost as much as you and your wife do," Dr. Meshew said.

George nodded. "She does," he said.

At the foot of the stairs, Mary Scally paused for a minute, lifted her head so she could see if Mr. Patton and the doctor were watching her, then, seeing that they weren't, headed not in the direction of the kitchen but toward the parlor instead.

When Georgie fretted, Mary kissed him and said, "I'll give you some sweet milk in a minute, my precious boy, but first, there is another important matter we have to take care of."

When Mary entered the parlor, a man standing at the fireplace turned toward her.

"We have to hurry, Father John," Mary said. "I don't want Mr. and Mrs. Patton to be angry with me."

"There should be no anger in making sure that their son's immortal soul is not prevented from entering heaven because he was never christened, Mary," Father John said. "I think you are doing the right thing."

While Mary held Georgie in her arms, Father John performed the christening ceremony, then he quietly slipped out a side door.

"Now, my sweet Georgie, no matter what happens, you will see Jesus, if our Savior decides to take you home sooner than we really want to part with you," Mary whispered into the baby's ears, "but before I take you back to your dear mother, I'm going to give you the milk that I promised."

To Mary's delight, Georgie took the milk that she offered him on her finger. Within days too, he began nursing his mother again, and soon everyone believed that the crisis had passed and that Georgie would indeed live to become the son his father had dreamed about.

One day, when George arrived home, he announced to Ruth that they were moving from Lake Vineyard to Los Angeles, so he could be closer to his work.

"But we'll still come out here on week-ends," George assured Ruth.

"I think you've made the right decision," Ruth said. What she didn't add was that she was also concerned about her husband's health. He was not a well man. She hoped that a shorter surrey ride each day would be less tiring for him.

A few months later, though, it was clear to both Ruth and George that De Barth Shorb, Ruth's brother-in-law, would soon have to declare bankruptcy. He had been in charge of the Wilson estate since her father's death but had mismanaged it. George agreed to give up his promising legal career to take over managing the business affairs of the estate. Once again, the Patton family moved back to Lake Vineyard. Georgie, now almost a year old, couldn't have been happier, and he seemed to grow healthier each day.

Lake Vineyard

By 1900, when Georgie was five, Lake Vineyard had two new wings that had been added to accommodate all of the family members who had decided to make it their permanent home. Besides Georgie's father and mother and his newborn sister, Nita, Georgie's grandmother Margaret Wilson still occupied the bedroom where his grandfather Don Benito had also lived. From time to time, when Grandmother Margaret was feeling well, she would tell Georgie thrilling stories about the grandfather he never knew. He never got tired of hearing them. The rest of the house was occupied by his aunt Nannie, his aunt Susie, and his aunt Nellie and her six children, as well as Nurse Scally, his and Nita's nanny.

The wood to build the additions had been cut from a forest that once covered the hillside behind the house. Georgie missed the trees, but he told himself that they were still with him. Instead of being on the hillside, though, they were now part of the house, and as such were probably happier being closer to such a wonderful family as his.

In front of the house was a wide, green lawn. On one side was an apple orchard. On the other side was a garden filled with all kinds of vegetables and flowers.

From time to time, friends from far away came to visit them, and they only added to the excitement Georgie felt at having so many people around. He enjoyed the constant attention he received.

One of Georgie's favorite rooms was the kitchen. Almost half of it was taken up by a fireplace that was used both for cooking and heating the house. He loved to sit in Mary Scally's lap and sip hot chocolate while she told him stories of Ireland.

"We had lots of horses in my country too, Georgie," Mary said. "When I was a very young girl, I'd gallop across the green country-side, ride to the edge of a cliff overlooking the Atlantic Ocean, and dream of America."

"Why would you do that, Mary?" Georgie asked. "Didn't you like Ireland?"

"Of course, I did, dearie, of course, I did. No Irishman or Irishwoman is ever anything but Irish, wherever he or she is finally laid to rest," Mary said, "but Ireland was a very poor land, then, and America held so much prom-ise for us."

"Are you glad you came to America?" Georgie asked her after a few minutes.

"Oh, yes, I am, dearie," Mary answered.

"I've never regretted it for one minute." She hugged him tight. "If I had never come to America, I should never have known you, my precious Georgie, and I can't imagine that, can you?"

Georgie grinned. "No," he said.

"Well, story time is over, Georgie," Mary said. "Your sister is probably awake now, and I must see that she's all right."

"I'm going up to the attic," Georgie said.

"That dusty place?" Mary said. She let out a sigh. "Well, all right, but first you go change out of those clothes."

Once he had changed his clothes, Georgie climbed the stairs that led to the attic. It really was a dusty place, just as Mary had said, but it was full of things that always gave him pleasant dreams, both day and night. There were books of all kinds, but Georgie especially liked the ones that had drawings of battles in them. He could stare at them for hours. He never pictured himself as one of the regular soldiers, though. He always saw himself as a general leading the other men into battle.

The attic was also full of saddles of all kinds, from the simplest to the most intricate, and one of Georgie's favorite games was deciding which one he would use for whatever battle he would be riding his horse into that day.

There were also swords that had belonged to various family members. When Georgie had asked about them, his father told him stories about which wars they had been used in. Most of the swords were from either the American Civil War or from the Mexican War, but some of them were from earlier wars that had been fought in faraway Europe. Often, Georgie would draw a sword from its scabbard, thrust it toward a pretend enemy, and then wonder what it would have been like for the real enemy to see this particular sword coming toward him in battle. Georgie knew that swords were no longer used in wars.

Instead, wars were fought with guns, and the attic also had plenty of those. As he did with the swords, Georgie would use the rifles in pretend battles. Often, though, he just liked to sit and admire the workmanship. He was amazed at how the wood had been carved, how the barrels had been fashioned, and how the mechanisms all worked to make an object of such beauty.

"I'll be a soldier one of these days," Georgie whispered. "I'll be the best soldier in the United States Army too."

Suddenly, a noise in the corner of the room startled Georgie, and he whipped his neck around. "Who's there?" he whispered.

When no one answered, he asked in a louder voice, "Is that you, Robert?"

Robert was one of his cousins, one of Aunt Nellie's sons, and for some reason he enjoyed trying to scare Georgie, but Georgie usually found a way to turn the tables on him. After a few minutes, when Robert didn't jump out and shout, "Boo!"—which always sent his cousin into hysterics—Georgie knew that it was probably one of the rats that lived there. Some of the other residents of Lake Vineyard complained about the rats, but because Georgie's parents believed the rats weren't really harming anyone, they wouldn't allow anyone to do anything except shoo them away. The same went for the family of skunks that lived under the house. These black-and-white "kittens" eventually found a hole next to the pipes in one of the inside bathrooms, which allowed them access to the room, and they used it so frequently that Mr. Patton cut a hole in the bathroom door so that the skunks would have access to the rest of the house. But Georgie, along with everyone else in the family, was cautioned not to pet the black-and-white "kittens."

Just then, Georgie heard another noise, but this was one that thrilled him more than almost any other sound: the whinnying of his father's horse, Apple. He rushed over to the attic window, brushed away some cobwebs, and looked out. Below him, in the backyard, Georgie saw his father astride the beautiful reddish-brown horse. Excitement surged through him.

Georgie immediately put everything away, then headed downstairs as fast as he could and out the back door. "Papa!" George cried.

Mr. Patton laughed. "I knew you'd be along shortly," he said. "I was sure that Apple was calling you with her neighs."

Georgie grinned. "I heard her, Papa," he said. "I could tell she was talking to me."

"Get on behind me, Georgie, and you can ride with me over to the corral," Mr. Patton said. "I have a surprise for you."

George took his father's hand and let himself be pulled up onto the saddle. As he held tightly to his father's waist, they headed in the direction of the corral.

When they reached it, Mr. Patton said,

"Well, Georgie, what do you think?"

Georgie stared in disbelief. In the corral, he saw what looked liked four full-grown horses, but they were half the normal size. "What are they, Papa?" he asked.

"Shetland ponies," Mr. Patton replied. "They're originally from islands off the coast of Great Britain, but there's a man near here who raises them, and I bought these four today." He dismounted, then helped Georgie down. "I'm giving one of them to you, Georgie. You can choose which one you want."

Georgie ran to the corral fence, climbed up, and sat down on the top log. Right away, one of the ponies came up to him. Georgie patted the pony's nose. He couldn't believe how soft it was.

"Here are some carrots, Georgie," Mr. Patton said. "See if she'll eat one from you."

Georgie held a carrot out to the pony. The pony took it from his hand and started eating it.

"What's her name, Papa?" Georgie asked.

"Peach Blossom," Mr. Patton replied.

"Peach Blossom," Georgie repeated. "I like that name." He turned to his father. "She's the one I want."

Mr. Patton smiled. "Somehow I had the feeling that you'd choose her," he said. "We'll saddle her up, and I'll lead you around the barn. How would you like that?"

"Oh, Papa, would you?" Georgie said.

For the next hour, Mr. Patton led Georgie around the barn in a slow gait, until Mrs. Patton came out to the barn and told them it was time for dinner. But Georgie didn't want to get off until he had shown his mother how he could "ride."

"That's wonderful, Georgie," Mrs. Patton said. "I'm sure it won't be long until I look out my window and see you galloping by."

"You may see me tomorrow, Mama," Georgie said.

"Oh, well, I think it'll be a while longer than that, Georgie," Mr. Patton said as he helped Georgie off Peach Blossom's back and handed the reins to one of the stable hands, "but I'm sure that time will be here before we know it."

True to his word, over the next few months, Mr. Patton began to take Georgie on longer rides around the estate, and soon Georgie was holding the reins himself. Now, Georgie's favorite place on the estate was no longer the attic but the stable. He loved the smell of the horses and the hay.

One night, after everyone had gone to bed, Georgie got out of bed, put his clothes back on, and quietly slipped downstairs and out the front door of the house.

"Polvo!" he called quietly. "Polvo!"

Within minutes, his dog came running up, wagging his tail and rubbing his head lovingly against Georgie's legs. Together, the two of them hurried across the wide lawn to the stables.

Georgie knew that some of the stable hands slept in rooms at the back, but he didn't think they'd hear him and Polvo, and even if they did, he had decided, the men worked for his father, so they wouldn't say anything to him about being in the stable this late at night.

The side doors to the stable were open, to let in the cool evening air. Inside, the light from the full moon helped them see where they were going.

At the opposite end of the stable, two horses Georgie had named Galahad and Marmion were in side-by-side stalls, and he and Polvo headed in that direction.

"Be quiet, Polvo," Georgie whispered. "We don't want to wake them if they're sleeping."

Georgie could tell from their breathing that the horses were asleep. Once in a while, a restless whinny would come from one of the stalls.

"Someone's dreaming," Georgie whispered to Polvo.

He suddenly wondered if horses dreamed of being in battles, like he did, and if they thought about the bravery of other horses, the way he thought about the bravery of other men.

After he had assured himself that the horses were all fine, he led Polvo to several bales of hay stacked in a corner, and together they lay down.

Georgie pulled a piece of straw out of the bale, stuck it in his mouth, and chewed on it for a while, then he patted Polvo's head and said, "I think I must be the happiest boy in the world."

Georgie stayed in the stable until the moon had almost set, then he trudged back into the house, up to his room, and got back into bed.

The next morning, Georgie awakened with a start and found Robert sitting on his bed.

"What do you want?" Georgie asked sleepily.

"I know a secret," Robert said.

"Well, I know a lot of secrets," Georgie told him, "so why do I care if you just know one?"

He turned over and closed his eyes, but Robert only moved to the other side of the bed.

"This one is about your aunt Annie," Robert said. He giggled. "The one you call Aunt *Nannie*."

Georgie opened his eyes. "What about her?" he said.

"I overheard Mama talking about her," Robert said. "She's in love with your papa."

Georgie sat up. "Get out of my room!" he said. "Get out of here now!"

Robert stuck out his lower lip. "What are you getting angry at me for?" he said. "I'm just telling you what I overheard Mama saying."

Georgie didn't say anything else, but he glared at Robert until he had left his room. Then he lay back down, thinking about what his cousin had said. Out of all his family members, the one person he didn't really understand was

Aunt Nannie. He loved her, but he sometimes thought that his aunt and his mother didn't really like each other. This was the first time that anyone had ever suggested the reason, though, and he wasn't quite sure what to think about it.

George knew how much his aunt Nannie adored him, and she was always smiling at his father, too, but Aunt Nannie never seemed to want his mother around, and Georgie noticed that she seldom paid any attention to his sister Nita. Aunt Nannie always took his side too. If he wanted to do something that his mother didn't want him to do, then Aunt Nannie made sure he did it. Once in a while, he thought he saw a frown on his mother's face when Aunt Nannie was around, but Georgie had never heard her say anything ill about her sister.

When Georgie was finally dressed, he went downstairs to breakfast. The family was already seated. Georgie noticed his mother raise an eyebrow, and he wondered if she would ask him why he looked as if he hadn't gotten much sleep, but before any words could come out of her mouth, Aunt Nannie said, "Here, my sweet Georgie, take your seat and I'll have the cook bring you some pancakes instead of mush today." Aunt Nannie looked around the room to see if anyone dared contradict her. "There's nothing too good for this child."

George took his seat. He had decided that it didn't really make any difference to him what Robert had said. He knew that as far as Aunt Nannie was concerned, he could do no wrong, and that was all he needed to know.

Nothing's Too Good
for Georgie

One bright morning in early June of 1893, when Georgie was seven, he decided to ride Galahad to a far edge of his family's estate, because Mary had told him that she knew there were some patches of wild strawberries in the area. She said that if Georgie would pick them for her, she would have the cook make some special strawberry jam that only the two of them would eat.

By now, Georgie was well on his way to

becoming an expert horseman. He knew how to take care of the animals, and he knew how to saddle up his horse without any help.

As Georgie headed away from the grounds of Lake Vineyard, with Polvo tagging along beside him, he rode first down a drive leading to a dirt road that, if he took it, would eventually lead him to the main road that went on into Los Angeles, but instead of turning right, he turned left.

Georgie thought he had a pretty good idea of where to look for the strawberries, because he was sure there was a stream nearby he had once gone wading in with some of his cousins.

As Georgie rode through the fields, passing from time to time underneath some of the larger trees that still dotted the landscape, he thought he could probably live at Lake Vineyard for the rest of his life and be a very happy person.

Suddenly, he stopped.

Ahead of him there were two long, horse-drawn wagons loaded with fence posts and barbed wire. At first, it was difficult for Georgie to comprehend what the men were doing, but after a moment he realized they were putting a fence across the Patton land.

Polvo barked.

"Hey!" Georgie shouted. "Stop that."

Quickly, he urged Galahad toward the wagons. First, he would confront the men, he had decided, then he would ride back to the house and tell his father what they were doing.

At Georgie's shout, the men had stopped what they were doing and looked at him.

When Georgie reached them, he reined in and said, "Why are you putting up a fence here? This is Patton land!"

One of the men stepped forward. "Who are you?" he asked.

"I'm George S. Patton, Jr., that's who," Georgie said. "My father owns this land."

The man smiled. "Well, he doesn't own

it anymore, son," he said. "I'm Joshua Framingham. I bought several hundred acres of this estate from your father, so it's my land now."

"Papa wouldn't sell this land, sir," Georgie insisted, but even he could tell by the tone of his voice that he was no longer sure. "He just wouldn't," Georgie added.

"Well, if I had it with me, young man, I'd show you the bill of sale, but you'll just have to take my word for it until you can talk to your father," Mr. Framingham said. "Now, me and my men need to get back to putting up this fence so we can let the cattle out to graze."

"But Mary wanted me to look for wild strawberries," Georgie protested.

At that, the men laughed. Georgie felt himself blushing deeply. Not waiting to see what Mr. Framingham would say about the strawberries, he turned Galahad around and raced back to the house. Polvo could barely keep up.

At the stable, Georgie asked one of the surprised stable hands if he would take care of
Galahad just this once, then he ran into the
house, calling, "Papa! Papa!"

Aunt Nannie intercepted him, pulled him
into her arms, and held him tight until he felt
himself relaxing.

"What or *who* has upset you, Georgie?"
Aunt Nannie demanded.

Georgie took a deep breath and told her.

"Come with me, Georgie," Aunt Nannie
said, taking Georgie's hand and leading him
into the parlor, where they sat next to each
other on one of the settees.

Georgie leaned his head on Aunt Nannie's
shoulder.

"My sweet child, he should have told you,
and I don't know why he didn't, but I'll tell
you now, because I think you should know
everything that is going on around you," Aunt
Nannie said. "Your father is a wonderful man,
Georgie, in fact, the most wonderful man in

the world, and you are his pride and joy. He would do anything for you, as would I, but his health isn't good, and that has kept him from being able to practice law in Los Angeles, so there is simply less money available than there used to be. Your father sold that land, which really isn't all that good, Georgie, no matter what that silly Mary thinks, so he could buy you a new rod and reel, because he's planning to take you fishing with him next week."

Georgie hugged his aunt Nannie. "Oh, isn't Papa just the most wonderful person in the world?" he said.

"Yes, he is, Georgie," Aunt Nannie said. "I've always thought that."

True to his word, Mr. Patton took Georgie fishing the next weekend. With a packhorse behind them, which carried a tent, camping supplies, and their fishing gear, they rode up to a lake in one of the nearby hills.

When they got to the place where Mr.

Patton wanted to camp, Georgie said, "Papa, do we own this land?"

"Yes, we do, Georgie," Mr. Patton replied. "Why do you ask?"

"I don't ever want you to sell it, no matter what," Georgie said. "I always want this to be a place where you and I can come to be alone."

Georgie noticed his father's Adam's apple bob a couple of times before Mr. Patton said, "That is a promise, son."

For the next hour, they unloaded their equipment, set up the tent, and gathered firewood.

Finally, when everything was ready, Mr. Patton said, "I think the fish will be biting now, Georgie, so let's go on down to the lake and find out."

"All right, Papa," Georgie said.

They gathered up their fishing rods and reels and set out for the lake, which was just down a short incline from their camp. Mr.

Patton was right: It didn't take either one of them very long to hook a fish.

"What kind of fish did I catch, Papa?" Georgie asked.

"It's a bass," Mr. Patton said as he showed him how to take it off the hook, "but if you'll look at the size of that mouth, you'll see it's pretty large, so it's called a *largemouth* bass."

Georgie held the fish in his two hands and said, "It's kind of slippery, Papa. What am I supposed to do with it?"

"That's why I brought that metal bucket along, son, and filled it with lake water," Mr. Patton said. "We'll put the fish in it until we're ready to go back to camp, so they'll stay alive."

Georgie dropped the fish into the bucket and then watched as Mr. Patton took his fish off the hook.

"That fish's mouth doesn't look as big as mine," Georgie said.

"Aha, you're very observant, son," Mr.

Patton said. "This one is called a *smallmouth* bass, but I can tell you that it's just as good to eat as yours!"

Georgie laughed. "Let's see how many more we can catch, Papa!" he said.

That night, they ate fried fish, corn bread, and leftover pinto beans that the cook had sent with them.

As Georgie helped himself to a third plateful of everything, Mr. Patton said, "It's this fresh air, son. It makes you hungry, doesn't it?"

Georgie nodded. "Yes, sir," he said, "it really does."

Later that night, as they lay together, on their backs, in the tent, the flap open so they could look at the stars, Georgie said, "Aunt Nannie said your health isn't very good, Papa. I don't want you to die, ever, because I couldn't live without you."

For a couple of minutes Mr. Patton didn't say anything, and Georgie could only hear his soft breathing, but then finally, he turned over on his side to face Georgie, ran his fingers through Georgie's hair, and said, "I don't feel well, from time to time, Georgie, but I'm not going to die, not anytime soon, that is, because I still have a lot of things I want to do for you."

"Oh, Papa, I'm so glad to hear you say that," Georgie said.

Within a few minutes, Georgie felt himself drifting off to sleep, knowing that no matter what happened in the rest of the world, his papa would always be there for him.

Mr. Patton continued to take Georgie fishing and hunting. Sometimes, they would be gone for several days, but often they would simply search out squirrels in the nearby trees and set traps for them. Often, they'd take the squirrels to the cook, who was then responsible for killing, skinning, and then frying them. But Georgie and Mr. Patton were about the only ones in the family who ate the squirrel meat, although Aunt Nannie would at least help herself to a small piece and then pick at it for a while.

"This is about all that some of our soldiers had when they were fighting the Indians on the frontier," Mr. Patton would tell everyone. "Why, if it hadn't been for squirrels, then this country wouldn't be what it is today!"

That was good enough for Georgie. "If I'm going to be a soldier, Papa," he announced, "then I need to eat what they eat!"

Whatever fish or game that Mr. Patton and Georgie brought home almost always found its way to the Pattons' table, but none of it was ever eaten on Sunday. That was considered the most formal meal of the week, and the meat served then came only from the butcher. Right before the family sat down at the table, Mr. Patton would go into his study, but the day after Georgie's eighth birthday, in

1893, Mr. Patton invited Georgie to accompany him.

"I always have a drink of whiskey before dinner, Georgie," Mr. Patton said, "and today I want you to have one too."

Mr. Patton opened a cupboard, took out a crystal decanter, and poured himself a large glass of whiskey. He poured Georgie a smaller one and then handed it to him.

"Have a seat, son, and let's enjoy our drink before dinner," Mr. Patton said.

Georgie sat down in a chair next to his father's. A small mahogany table was between them. Georgie brought the glass to his mouth, sniffed the contents, then set it back down. He thought it smelled horrible.

"It's an acquired taste, Georgie, but all men drink whiskey, so this is something you need to get used to," his father told him. "This liquor cabinet is never locked, and you can get a drink from it whenever you want one."

"Thank you, Papa," Georgie said.

Once again, Georgie picked up the glass and lifted it to his mouth, but this time he let his tongue touch the brown liquid. It burned something awful, he thought, but he wanted to show his father that he was a man, so he allowed a little more of the whiskey to come into his mouth, then he closed his eyes and swallowed it. It burned all the way down his throat and continued to burn for several seconds once it reached his stomach, but then after a few more seconds, the burning went away and Georgie felt a funny, warm sensation all the way through his body. He had never felt so strange before.

Georgie managed to down about half of the contents of his glass before his father set his empty glass on the table and said, "It's time we go to dinner, son."

Georgie stood up, then sat back down as his head began to spin. His father was already headed toward the door and hadn't noticed that Georgie was having trouble getting his bearings. Georgie tried to stand up again, and this time he managed to stay up and follow his father to the dinning room, where the rest of the family were waiting for them, but he still felt light-headed.

When Mr. Patton and Georgie were seated, Mr. Patton said the blessing, and then the food was served, but for some reason, nothing looked good to Georgie, including the roast beef and mashed potatoes, which he had been looking forward to.

Later that day, sitting with Aunt Nannie in the parlor, Georgie asked her why his father had wanted him to drink whiskey.

"I've never tasted anything so awful," Georgie said.

"Georgie, you may find that later in life you'll welcome a glass of whiskey," Aunt Nannie said, "but your father simply wants you to understand that drinking is not something he forbids you to do, and since it isn't forbidden, he doesn't want you sneaking off somewhere to drink by yourself, which quite often happens in families where spirits are hidden from the young people."

Georgie looked at her in surprise. "I don't understand, Aunt Nannie," he said.

"Well, I frequently have a glass of your father's whiskey, Georgie, because he doesn't like to drink alone, and your mother certainly isn't going to join him," Aunt Nannie said. "This way, your father is telling you that you, too, may join him, whenever you wish, but that it will always be your decision."

All of a sudden, Georgie remembered those occasions when he had seen his aunt Nannie coming out of his father's study, a glass in her hand, similar to the one into which his father had poured Georgie's whiskey. He had been told to leave Aunt Nannie alone when she wasn't feeling well, and it always seemed to him that those were the times when she didn't seem like the woman he loved so much. Although she never said a harsh or unkind word to Georgie, she yelled at other people, blaming them for everything that was wrong with the world around her. Usually, Georgie left the house and went to the stable until things had quieted down. No one ever complained about Aunt Nannie's outbursts, though. The family just seemed to accept them.

But Georgie knew that his father didn't act that way when he drank whiskey. If he ever decided to take up drinking, he hoped that he would be like his father instead of like his aunt Nannie.

"Do you want me to read to you, Georgie?" Aunt Nannie asked.

Georgie nodded. No one else read to him as much as Aunt Nannie did.

"Well, what shall it be, then?" Aunt Nannie asked. She stood up and went to the large bookcase. "We could continue with some of the classics, like the *Odyssey* or the *Iliad*, but your father asked me to let him finish those, so I think we should grant him his wish, don't you?"

"Yes, ma'am," Georgie replied.

Aunt Nannie picked up the family Bible from off a table next to the fireplace and said, "Let's read from the most exciting book that has ever been written, Georgie."

Georgie smiled. "All right," he said.

Aunt Nannie returned to her seat, and Georgie prepared to spend the next several hours enthralled by her voice.

"The Bible is the most noble tale of man's survival, Georgie," Aunt Nannie said. "And Jesus is the example of human courage that we should all follow."

As Georgie lay with his head on Aunt Nannie's shoulder, he began to twirl a long strand of his hair around his fingers. He didn't know why he did it, but for some reason, it comforted him.

All of a sudden, Aunt Nannie stood up and

said, "Georgie, you simply have to break that habit. It gets on my nerves, sweetheart."

"I'm sorry, Aunt Nannie," Georgie said.

"Let's get down on our knees and ask God's forgiveness for all of our sins, before we start reading His word," Aunt Nannie said. "Prayer should always precede any of the other things we do in life, Georgie, and I hope you never forget that."

Aunt Nannie knelt in front of the settee, and Georgie knelt beside her.

"I'll never forget about God and Jesus, Aunt Nannie," Georgie said. "No matter where I am, I'll always remember to talk to them."

Heroes and Battles

By the time that Georgie was nine years old, in 1894, horses and horsemanship had become second nature to him. He could often be seen galloping around the grounds of Lake Vineyard on either Galahad or Marmion, the wind whipping his blond curls in every direction, and Polvo running close behind.

On many days, Aunt Nannie would be sitting out on the front porch so she could wave at him whenever he passed. From time to time, Georgie would see Nita and his cousins doing various chores around the estate, but it never occurred to him that he should be helping them. After all, he was George Smith Patton, Jr., the scion of the Patton family and, as such, wasn't expected to do anything but grow up and bring more glory to the Patton name.

One November evening, after a full day of riding around the estate, pretending to be some of the heroes in the books he loved so much, Georgie went to Aunt Nannie's room, knocked, then, when there was no answer, opened it slightly and saw Aunt Nannie, dressed in her nightgown, propped up against several pillows.

"What's wrong, Aunt Nannie?" Georgie whispered.

"Come closer, my precious boy," Aunt Nannie whispered. "I have something to tell you."

With a pounding heart, Georgie crept across the rug to the edge of the bed. Aunt Nannie reached out her hand, and Georgie took it.

"I don't know how much longer I'll live, Georgie," Aunt Nannie said, her voice barely audible, "but I want to tell you how much I love you, and I want you to promise me faithfully that you'll always obey your dear father, because he has been God's gift to this family."

Georgie swallowed hard. "I promise, Aunt Nannie, but you can't leave me, because . . ."

"Georgie!"

Georgie turned and saw his mother standing at the door.

"You need to go now, son," Mrs. Patton said. "You don't need to be disturbing your aunt."

"He's not disturbing me, Susan!" Aunt Nannie said.

Georgie thought her voice sounded stronger all of a sudden.

"Georgie! Please do as I say!" Mrs. Patton said. "I have to give your aunt Nannie her medicine."

"I'm not taking any of your medicine,

Susan," Aunt Nannie said. "I'm already beginning to feel better."

Georgie wasn't exactly sure what was going on between his mother and his aunt, but he decided that it might be better if he obeyed his mother this time rather than wait until his aunt had argued to get his way.

Once outside Aunt Nannie's room, he thought for a minute about putting his ear up against the door, to hear what his mother and Aunt Nannie might be saying to each other, but his cousin Robert came along just then.

"Have you seen Papa?" Georgie asked him.

"I saw him go into his study with another man," Robert said. He gave Georgie a sly grin. "I know what he does when he goes in there either alone or with other people."

Georgie gave Robert a steely stare. "I do too," he said. "He chooses the books that he's going to read me before bedtime."

"That's not what Mama says he does," Robert countered.

"Well, your mama's a liar," Georgie said, "and if she doesn't stop saying those things about Papa, then I'm going to tell her to move."

"You can't do that," Robert said.

"I can," Georgie said. "I will!"

Georgie watched as Robert scurried down the corridor and was soon out of sight, then he headed for his father's study, curious as to who their new guest was.

When he got there, the door was closed, always a sign to everyone else that Mr. Patton was not to be disturbed, but Georgie knew that that didn't apply to him.

He knocked loudly and said, "It's Georgie, Papa!" and then opened the door and went inside.

Mr. Patton and a man he had never seen before at Lake Vineyard were standing together in front of the fireplace, drinks in hand, as Georgie entered the room.

"Ah, Georgie, I was hoping you were somewhere close by, because I want you to meet

Colonel John Singleton Mosby," Mr. Patton said.

"Colonel Mosby! It's an honor to meet you, sir," Georgie said. He and Colonel Mosby shook hands. "I know all about you from what Papa has told me."

"Well, it's an honor to meet you, too, Georgie," Colonel Mosby said.

Mr. Patton pulled up a third chair, poured Georgie a small drink, and said, "At this time of the evening, John, I usually read to Georgie. He likes to hear about great warriors in famous battles. We've read the *Odyssey* and the *Iliad*. We've read stories of Alexander the Great, Plutarch's *Lives*, and Xenophon's *The Persian Expedition*."

"Don't forget about Napoleon, Papa," Georgie said.

"Yes. Napoleon," Mr. Patton said. "And on many an evening we've also talked about those great men in our Confederacy who tried to save the South."

"General Stonewall Jackson, General Robert E. Lee, my own grandfather, Colonel George Smith Patton," Georgie said. He grinned. "*And*, of course, Colonel John Singleton Mosby."

Mr. Patton nodded. "But tonight, Georgie, you won't have to hear these stories second-hand," he said. "Colonel Mosby has agreed to tell you in his own words about the raids he led during the Civil War."

"Oh, thank you, sir," Georgie said. "This is such an honor for me."

Georgie took a sip of the whiskey. Just one sip, because he still couldn't stand the taste, but he didn't want Colonel Mosby to think he wasn't a man.

With the fire crackling, with the remembrance of how he had spent the day, racing Galahad around the estate, in search of enemy soldiers, Georgie leaned back, thrilled that he had been born into a family where evenings could be spent listening to true heroes.

For the next two hours, Colonel Mosby regaled Georgie and Mr. Patton with his daring exploits.

In the late summer of 1864 Colonel Mosby prevented a Union victory in the northern and western parts of Virginia, but the road to that victory hadn't been easy. In 1861 at the beginning of the war, Mosby was a private in the Virginia Cavalry. By the end of the war, he was a colonel.

In 1862 Mosby was given the authority to raise a band of partisans, irregular soldiers, whose only job was to wreak havoc among the Union supply lines so that the commanders would have to dispatch large numbers of troops to guard these facilities. Sometimes, Mosby's soldiers would disguise themselves as the enemy, which allowed them to infiltrate Union positions. He and his men were so successful at frustrating the Union troops that large bounties were placed on their heads, and when the partisans were caught, they were executed on the spot rather than imprisoned. When General Robert E. Lee surrendered in 1865, officially ending the war, Mosby simply disbanded his command so he wouldn't have to surrender officially. He wasn't pardoned until 1866.

After the war, Mosby returned to his law practice. He also became a friend of one of the Confederacy's biggest enemies, General Ulysses S. Grant, whom he supported in the presidential elections of 1868 and 1872. A lot of Mosby's friends in the South despised him for that, but he was rewarded with several government posts.

"I won't lie to you, Georgie," Colonel Mosby said as he ended his story. "It was a difficult decision for me to become friends with Grant, but a soldier's duty is always to his commander in chief, and those Southerners who are still fighting the Civil War aren't not true Americans, in my opinion."

Georgie had never heard anyone voice such

an opinion before, but coming from Colonel Mosby, it all made sense. It was a soldier's duty to carry out his orders, and no matter how many officers there were in the military chain of command, the president of the United States was where it all ended.

Later that night, after Colonel Mosby had gone to bed, Georgie went in to tell Mama and Papa good night.

His mother was standing in front of a mirror, brushing her hair. He gave her one kiss, then said, "Good night, Mama."

"Good night, Georgie," Mrs. Patton said. "I think you need to stay in your room tonight."

Georgie felt himself blushing. He had no idea his mother knew that from time to time he still slipped out of the house so he could lie in the hay in the stable with his beloved horses.

"Yes, ma'am, Mama," Georgie said.

Mr. Patton was sitting up in bed, reading a

newspaper, when Georgie walked over to him and sat on the edge.

"Thank you for letting me visit with Colonel Mosby, Papa," he said.

"He's a Southern hero, Georgie," Mr. Patton said. "There aren't many of those left."

Georgie gave his papa a big hug and kissed him several times. In a soft voice, he whispered, "Take care of yourself, Papa. I don't want anything to happen to you."

Mr. Patton looked up. "Why would anything happen to me?" he whispered back.

"You work so hard, trying to give us all the things we want, trying to keep us out of the poorhouse," Georgie said.

"You've been listening to your aunt Nannie again, haven't you?" Mr. Patton said.

"Well, she's always worrying about you, Papa," Georgie said. "I'm sure that's why she was so sick tonight, just thinking about all the things you do to make the family happy."

"Well, I'm still not going to die anytime

soon, Georgie, no matter what your aunt Nannie might believe," Mr. Patton said.

"I don't want you to sell Apple, either, Papa," Georgie said. "Even if we have to go without food, we should never get rid of that stallion."

Mr. Patton ruffled Georgie's hair. "Are you sure you're not more worried about that horse than you are about me?" he whispered.

"Oh, no, Papa," Georgie assured him.

"Well, then go on to bed," Mr. Patton said, "and remember what your mother said: No sneaking out of the house."

"Yes, Papa," Georgie said. He kissed his father one more time, then left the room.

One of Georgie's favorite heroes was King John, who ruled Bohemia—which is now part of the Czech Republic—from 1310 until his death in 1346. King John spent his life fighting battles that would bring him glory. During one of those campaigns, in 1337, he was blinded, but even that didn't stop him from fighting. He died during the Battle of Crécy, heroically charging British archers, who cut him down in a hail of arrows. Georgie had always thought that there could be no greater honor than to die that way for one's country. He often dreamed of what it would have been like to be King John.

One morning, after such a dream, Georgie decided that on this day he would re-enact one of King John's famous campaigns. In several battles, King John had taken an ordinary horse-drawn supply wagon and fitted it with a metal top and metal sides with narrow slits. His men could shoot their arrows out of the slits and stay protected behind the impenetrable metal. Georgie wanted to build an armored wagon like he had seen in his dreams.

With four of his cousins in tow, he headed for a large barn, almost half a mile from the house.

"I still don't understand how you're going

to do it," Robert complained. "It sounds kind of complicated to me."

Georgie pointed to his head. "It's all up here," he said.

When they reached the barn, Georgie pointed to a wagon that was often used to haul barrels of wine into town.

"That's what we need," he said. "Now, all we have to do is turn it into an *armored* wagon."

"Won't Uncle George get angry?" Louisa asked.

"Of course, he won't," Georgie said. "He lets me do whatever I want."

For the next several minutes they all looked around the barn, trying to find pieces of metal that they could attach to the sides of the wagon, but there was nothing Georgie thought would work.

"I know what we'll do," Georgie said finally. "We'll use the tops of some wine barrels. No arrows can penetrate this wood."

Everyone agreed that the wine barrel tops

would do. They went through the barn, taking the tops off all the discarded barrels. Using hammers and nails, they built the sides of the armored wagon.

"I don't know if this will work or not, Georgie," Julia said. "Those barrel tops are round, so some of the arrows might come in through the places where they don't cover."

Georgie shook his head. "It's perfect, Julia," he said. "We need those openings so we can shoot our arrows through them, but when the enemy is shooting arrows at us, we'll just get behind the barrel tops."

"Who's the enemy?" Louisa asked.

"Mama's turkeys," Georgie replied.

"Whoever heard of a turkey being an enemy, Georgie?" Julia asked. "Couldn't it be somebody else?"

Georgie shook his head. "I've worked it all out strategically, Julia," he said.

"I wish you wouldn't use words that I don't know," Louisa complained.

"What I mean is that I've planned out this battle already," Georgie said. "It's all about positioning your troops so they have the most advantage, and that's what I've done."

Georgie explained to his cousins that where they were, at the top of a hill behind their house, gave them the upper hand over the enemy flock of turkeys whose encampment lay at the bottom.

"We'll push the wagon to the edge," Georgie said, "then we'll all get inside and ride down for a surprise attack."

"Won't the turkeys see us?" Louisa asked. "Won't they know we're coming?"

Georgie shook his head. "This is a *night* battle, Julia, and the turkeys are not expecting the attack."

Finally, the wagon was ready. Julia and Louisa climbed on. Robert and Georgie got behind, gave the wagon a shove and, as it began rolling down the hill, jumped on themselves.

Julia and Louisa immediately started screaming. Robert looked over at Georgie, who could see the fear on his face.

Georgie wasn't afraid, though. There was nothing frightening about going into battle. Still, the wagon was going a bit faster than he had imagined it would. In fact, he was quite sure that it wouldn't stop at the edge of the pen where he'd planned for them to shoot their pretend arrows at the turkeys.

It didn't.

The wagon picked up even more speed and plowed right through the fence and into the middle of the flock, massacring several of the enemy.

Feathers flew everywhere. The surviving turkey enemies were making frightened gobbling sounds and trying to figure out a way to escape.

Georgie looked at his cousins' terrified faces, then he surveyed the slain turkeys, whose bodies seemed to be everywhere.

"I think we won the battle," Georgie said tentatively.

Just then, they heard several shouts coming from the house. Georgie turned and saw his mother, his father, and his aunts Nannie and Nellie running toward them.

"What in the world happened here?" Mrs. Patton demanded.

Georgie explained the steps leading up to his military victory.

"George Smith Patton, Jr.! This time, you've gone too far!" Mrs. Patton said. "I want you to march up to the house right now and wait for me in your room. You will be punished!"

"Now, now, Susan," Mr. Patton said. "It looks as though no one was hurt, and boys will be boys, so I don't think—"

"George, I will not be deterred this time," Mrs. Patton said. "Georgie has to be taught a lesson."

"Oh, my heart! My heart!" Aunt Nannie cried.

Georgie watched his mother first look at Aunt Nannie, then at Aunt Nellie. "Nellie, please go summon the doctor, then turn down Annie's bed, for I do believe she's having another one of her attacks."

"Yes, Susan," Aunt Nellie said. She turned to Louisa, Julia, and Robert. "Do you care to come with me now?"

Georgie watched his cousins disappear up the hill. Finally, he turned to look at his mother. He knew this time, nothing his father or his aunt Nannie could say would help him.

Santa Catalina

One July morning in 1895, when Georgie was ten, Mr. Patton announced at breakfast, "We're going to Catalina tomorrow."

Everyone at the table cheered.

Georgie loved Santa Catalina Island. He knew that people have been drawn to it for thousands of years. Just twenty miles off the coast of Southern California, Catalina, as most people called it, had a colorful history, and Georgie knew it almost by heart.

In 1542, when Juan Rodriguez Cabrillo claimed the island for Spain, it was already populated with a group of Uto-Aztecan Indians who had migrated from what is present-day Nevada, Utah, and California. They lived off the island's plant life and fished the surrounding waters. Over the next several hundred years, the island was ruled by Spain, Mexico, California, and, when California became a state, the United States. Thousands of people went there to seek their fortunes. Catalina saw explorers, ranchers, miners, sea otter hunters, and soldiers from Spain, Mexico, and finally the United States.

In 1892 the island was sold to the wealthy Banning family, who were relatives of the Pattons. The Bannings formed the Santa Catalina Island Company. They built roads, installed the first telephone and wireless telegraph systems, and built several tourist attractions, including two dance pavilions, a bandstand, an aquarium, a Greek amphitheater, and a golf course. They offered fishing excursions, sightseeing by stagecoach, and glass-bottom-boat trips. Catalina soon became the playground for the wealthy families of Southern California, and Georgie's father, wanting to make sure that his family was included in that group of people, bought land and built a cottage. It wasn't the largest house on the island, but it wasn't the smallest, either.

Since the Pattons always kept the cottage supplied with necessities, there was never a need to pack anything other than a few personal items, so by the next morning, everyone was ready. Three buggies were waiting outside the front entrance of the house, the luggage already inside, for the trip to Long Beach, where they would board the boat that would take them to Santa Catalina.

Georgie sat beside his father, who always insisted on driving the buggy he was in.

"Are you looking forward to the trip, Georgie?" Mr. Patton asked.

"Oh, yes, Papa," Georgie replied. "I love going to Catalina."

"We'll do all the things we like to do together, Georgie. Hunt and fish and swim," Mr. Patton said. "It'll just be you and me."

Georgie wanted to tell his father that they could just spend their time swimming in the ocean, if he wanted, because he had learned from his aunt Nannie that his father didn't really like hunting or fishing. He only did it because he thought that it was important for a gentleman to know those skills. But Georgie was afraid of hurting his father's feelings, so he decided not to say anything.

When they arrived in Long Beach, the drivers helped load the luggage onto the boat.

Today, the trip was smooth, although Georgie could remember times when the water had been really rough and several of the women had gotten seasick. He was proud that that had never happened to him.

Finally, Georgie said, "Look, Papa! There's Avalon!"

The town of Avalon was on the northeast

side of the island, in a beautiful sheltered valley, with a wide, crescent-shaped harbor. Georgie knew that its name came from the epic poem *Idylls of the King*, by Alfred, Lord Tennyson, which Aunt Nannie had read to him many times. In his mind, Georgie could see King Arthur, as he lay dying, saying that he would be going to Avalon, the beautiful island valley, where he would heal himself of his wounds.

When their boat finally arrived in Avalon, the harbor was full of sailboats and schooners of all sizes. To Georgie, Catalina always seemed like a magical land, rising out of the blue ocean, and he could hardly wait to partake of all the adventures the island held.

When everything was put away and the family had eaten dinner, Georgie was ready to explore, but he decided he was too tired to go far, so he walked by himself down to the harbor area and watched the sailboats. He made up stories about who the people in all the boats were and where they were going. When he got back to the house, his father was standing on the porch, his hands behind his back. "I've been looking all over for you, Georgie," he said. "I have a surprise for you!"

"Oh, Papa!" Georgie cried. "What is it?"

From behind his back, Mr. Patton produced a shotgun. "It has a sixteen-gauge hammer, Georgie," he said. "We're going up into the hills tomorrow to hunt wild goat, then we're going to have a goat roast when we get back."

Georgie took the shotgun from his father and examined it. He could tell that it was expensive, and he knew that his father had probably sold off more of the estate just to have the money for it and for the trip to Catalina.

"I love it, Papa," Georgie said. "I really do."

"There is nothing too good for you, Georgie," Mr. Patton said. "I always want you to remember that."

"Thank you, Papa," Georgie said.

That night, Georgie slept with the rifle next to him. He could smell the wood and the oil from the barrel, and it made him feel safe and loved.

The next morning, Georgie was the first one awake. He was already sitting at the breakfast table when Mr. Patton came in. Instead of the mush they usually had back at Lake Vineyard, the cook had prepared a large breakfast of ham, eggs, toast, and strawberry jam.

When Mr. Patton raised an eyebrow, the cook said, "If you're going hunting, Mr. Patton, you and Georgie need a hearty breakfast, something more than mush, so there's no use in arguing with me!"

Georgie looked at his father, expecting him to scold the cook, but instead he only winked at Georgie and said, "With so much food to fortify us, Georgie, we'll probably be expected to bring back a whole herd of goats!"

Just as they finished eating, the other

members of the hunting party arrived. They were friends of Georgie's father's from Los Angeles, as well as three men called bearers whose job it was to carry the goats back to the cottage. Georgie saw that he was the only young boy, but that didn't matter to him because it meant he'd get all of the attention. When he showed everyone his new shotgun, they all asked to hold it, and when they returned it to him, they did so with their compliments.

"You'll probably shoot more goats than the rest of us combined," one man said.

Georgie grinned. "I'm ready to do that, gentlemen!" he said.

Georgie knew that the goats on the island had once been tame but had either escaped or had been let loose by their previous owners over the centuries, and that they offered residents and visitors alike a source of delicious meat, especially when they were roasted on a spit over an open fire. Just thinking about that made Georgie's mouth water.

For the next two hours, Georgie and the men climbed up and down the rugged hills, seeing signs of goats but not seeing any of the animals. It was Georgie who spotted the first prey.

"Look!" Georgie whispered. "I see a goat grazing on the other side of that bush."

"He's yours, then," Mr. Patton said.

Slowly, they crept closer until finally Georgie put up his hand and said, "I can get it from here."

He put the rifle to his shoulder and aimed. The bullet dropped the goat in its tracks.

Within the next two hours, every member of the hunting party, including Mr. Patton, had each killed one goat, but Georgie had killed four more.

When they got back to the cottage, the family and some of the neighbors had assembled to see what success the hunters had had.

The bearers laid the goats out on tables so they could start skinning and gutting them.

As everyone crowded around for a closer look, Georgie shouted, "I killed five of them! I killed more than anyone else did!"

Everyone smiled and nodded, but Mr. Patton pulled Georgie aside and said, "Son, it would have been more like a true sportsman not to have mentioned those extra goats."

Georgie bowed his head. "I'm sorry I bragged, Papa."

"The Pattons are gentlemen, Georgie, and gentlemen never brag in public," Mr. Patton said. "Will you promise me that you'll always remember that?"

Georgie knew his father was right, but he also knew himself, and he wondered just how difficult it would be to keep his word not only for the rest of the summer at Catalina but also when they returned to the mainland in September. But, still, he said, "I promise, Papa."

For the remainder of his time on Catalina, Georgie was able to keep his word, but right before his family's return to the mainland, it was sorely tested when the Pattons were invited to Hancock Banning's large home overlooking Avalon Harbor for dinner.

"I know your birthday isn't for a couple more months, Georgie," Hancock told him, "but I have a surprise for you, and I don't want to wait until November."

"I love surprises, Hancock," Georgie said to his cousin.

After dinner, everyone went out onto the veranda, which overlooked the harbor, and waited expectantly for Hancock's surprise.

Suddenly, fireworks of all colors lit up the sky, producing a spectacular scene below them.

When it was over, Georgie said, "You did this for *me*, Hancock?"

Hancock hugged Georgie, ruffled his golden curls, and said, "Nothing is too good for George Smith Patton, Jr."

"Thank you so much, Hancock," Georgie

said. He looked over at his father, who was beaming with pride, and said, "I hope everyone else enjoyed this as much as I did."

Everyone applauded.

"What a young gentleman," Aunt Nannie said. "He's a Patton through and through."

Georgie's Not Dumb!

Georgie knew that his father was haunted by the memories of his time at the Virginia Military Institute. It was a place obsessed with the chivalry that its graduates had shown during the Civil War. Often, whenever Mr. Patton was reading to Georgie, he would stop in the middle of a sentence, look over Georgie's shoulder as though he were staring at some distant horizon, beyond which lay the enemy, and say something about VMI's professors, its officers, its cadets, and its dead graduates. Mr. Patton would tell how his own father had been as heroic in battle as the characters about whom he had just been reading.

When Georgie asked his aunt Nannie about it, she told him that more than anything else in the world, Mr. Patton had wanted to follow his own father into military service, but that after graduation, he came back to California because he knew it was his responsibility to take care of his mother and his younger brother and sisters. Instead, he had handed off all his dreams of glory and his father's sword to Georgie, and it would be Georgie, Mr. Patton believed, who would bring the honor and glory to the Patton name on the field of battle.

Georgie, listening to Aunt Nannie tell him this, wrapped in the warmth of her arms, vowed that he would not disappoint his father, but one day in June of 1896, when Georgie was eleven, he was suddenly made to realize that he might not be smart enough to achieve what his father wanted for him.

"Sometimes I really do believe you're dim-witted, Georgie," Aunt Nannie said. "I've been reading to you since you were born, but you don't seem to be taking any of this in."

Georgie, who could smell liquor on Aunt Nannie's breath, said, "Yes, ma'am, I am, I swear."

"Well, by now you should be able to recognize at least some of the words in the Bible, Georgie," Aunt Nannie protested, "but every time I point to a word I've just read and ask you to repeat it, you aren't able to."

"I hear you when you say it, Aunt Nannie," Georgie said, "but when I look at it, it just doesn't look like what you said."

"Oh, that is such nonsense, such a poor excuse, Georgie," Aunt Nannie said. She took a deep breath and let it out gradually. "But we can't disappoint your father, so let's try again."

Georgie felt terrible. Worse, he felt dumb. No matter how hard he tried, he could never get the words on a page to make sense. One morning, Georgie overheard his parents talking about the problem.

"We'll simply tutor him at Lake Vineyard," Mrs. Patton said. "Heaven knows, Annie reads to him all the time from the classics, as do you, so he'll be schooled much as you were." Georgie heard his mother sniff a couple of times. "I just wish I understood what was wrong with him. Still, I think we're doing the right thing, George," Mrs. Patton continued. "If we send him to a regular school, he'll just be scorned by his classmates."

"I guess you're right, dear," Mr. Patton said.

For the rest of that day, Georgie thought about what he had heard. He had known for a long time that something was wrong—that, in a way he wasn't normal, like Nita or his cousins—but until now, he had just thought he was "special." It never occurred to him that he might be less intelligent than they were.

For the first time in his life he saw darkness all around him, and he didn't know how to get through it. He thought of one place he could go, where he could think better.

With Polvo, he hurried out to the stable and was happy when he saw that none of the stable hands were around. Galahad was lying down when he entered the horse's stall. He let Galahad nuzzle him, then leaned his head against the horse and cried.

When Georgie was spent, he lay with his back up against Galahad and thought about where his life would go from here. What was wrong with him? he wondered. He didn't even know where to start, so he decided to think about what a typical day was like. Sometimes, it was hard for him to concentrate, and he knew that he couldn't keep still, because quite often that's what people would say to him. "Concentrate, Georgie! And for heaven's sake, keep still!" So he would practice trying to concentrate, and he would consciously keep still.

What else? he wondered. He swallowed hard. He had never wanted to admit this, even to himself, but yes, he often felt inferior around other people his age, even stupid, but no one had ever said as much to him, because they knew he would fight anyone who did. "I won't feel that way anymore," he told Galahad, who neighed as if he understood. "I just won't feel that way anymore." He tried to think of other things. Suddenly, he remembered that Robert liked to tease him by moving things around in his room. "Why are you so neat, Georgie?" Robert would ask him. "You have everything lined up in rows." If Georgie put things back in order, Robert would just move them around again until Georgie chased him out of his room. *There's nothing wrong with being neat,* Georgie thought. *I like things in order, but I won't say anything about it to anyone.*

"I will prove to everyone that I'm not dumb, Galahad," Georgie said. "I will make them all proud of me!"

But then the darkness returned. "I'll just be fooling people, Galahad, I know I will," Georgie sobbed, the tears rolling down his cheeks, "and if I do succeed, it'll just be because I'm lucky."

Georgie lay with his head on Galahad for a while, until he felt as though he could face his family again, then he slowly stood up, patted Galahad, and left the stall.

When he got back to the house, his father was the first person he saw. "Oh, there you are, Georgie," Mr. Patton said. "I've been looking all over for you."

"I was in the stable with Galahad, Papa," Georgie said. "What's wrong?"

"I just wanted to tell you that Bishop Johnson is coming," Mr. Patton said, "and I'm sure he'll want to see you because he's always thought you were special, so why don't you put on something more presentable?"

"All right, Papa," Georgie said.

Now, the darkness was even deeper. The

Pattons were staunch Episcopalians, who went to church every Sunday. Georgie knew his father tithed by giving 10 percent of his earnings, even when they had very little money, but that's what good Episcopalians did. Don Benito, Georgie knew, had helped build some of the first Protestant churches in California, and Mr. Patton continued that tradition by serving on the churches' building committees.

From time to time, Bishop Johnson would put his arm around Georgie and say, "You would make a fine bishop one of these days, if you get the call, son, so keep your ears open for what God has to say to you."

To Georgie, hearing this was like a nightmare, and he felt guilty when he prayed to God not to call him to be the bishop of California. He always opened his prayer with, "I love you, God, but please don't call me, because I want to be a soldier."

When Bishop Johnson arrived, Georgie was

dressed to greet him, having told himself that he would concentrate and that he would keep still and that if Bishop Johnson mussed his hair, he wouldn't immediately run to his room and re-comb it, and by the end of the day, he felt he had achieved his goal. He was also quite happy when Bishop Johnson mentioned that the son of one of the other members of their church had told him that he wanted one day to be bishop of California.

"You have competition, Georgie," Bishop Johnson said. "You'll need to pray a little harder if you hope to get the call."

"I really do think that God wants me to be a soldier, Bishop Johnson," Georgie said.

"Well, God needs soldiers, too, Georgie," Bishop Johnson said.

At that moment, Georgie heard a voice in his head say, "You're smart! You're just as smart as anyone else! Don't ever forget that!"

Georgie looked around him to see if anyone was watching, for he was sure that if they were, they could tell that something wonderful was happening, because the feelings he had were so powerful. He would be a great warrior one of these days, he suddenly knew. He would prove himself worthy of his Patton heritage. Now, he knew, no one could stop him!

Classical School for Boys

On the morning of August 27, 1897, Georgie awakened to the sound of angry voices outside his room. At first, he thought he was still dreaming, but then he recognized his father's voice.

"What's wrong with you two? You can't protect him forever! He's almost twelve years old!" Mr. Patton shouted. "It's time for him to spread his wings."

"He's still in the nest, George!" Aunt Nannie

cried. "He's not ready to fly away!"

"Oh, for goodness' sakes," Mr. Patton said.

"I have to agree with Annie, George," Mrs. Patton said. "I just don't think that Georgie is ready for—"

"I say he's ready, so he's ready," Mr. Patton said, interrupting her. "When classes start in September, Georgie will be there."

Georgie waited for several minutes, then, when he could no longer hear voices outside his room, he got out of bed, dressed, and went downstairs to the dining room, where everyone was already seated for breakfast.

His father looked up at him and smiled. "Well, sleepyhead, I thought I was going to have to come get you," he said.

"Good morning, Georgie," his mother said, but Georgie could tell that she was unhappy.

Suddenly, Aunt Nannie stood up and clutched her heart. "I don't think I'm going to make it this time, I really don't!" she cried.

"Will somebody please help me to my room and then call the doctor? I've left instructions for my funeral in the second drawer of my chest, so it should be easy on . . ."

"Annie, please sit down," Mr. Patton said calmly. "This is no time for you to die."

Aunt Nannie blinked, opened her mouth in astonishment, clutched her heart, put her hand in her pocket and withdrew a handkerchief, which she used to wipe her brow, and then sat back down.

"It was just one of my spells, but thank goodness it wasn't a bad one," Aunt Nannie said, "so I guess I'm going to be all right this time, but the end will come, one of these days. . . ." She trailed off, lifting a spoonful of mush to her mouth.

When Georgie was seated, the cook served him his mush, then hurried back into the kitchen.

"Will you play with me after breakfast, Georgie?" Nita asked, looking up from her mush. "You don't play with me much any-more."

"Georgie and I have some things to discuss, Nita," Mr. Patton said.

"We'll play with you, Nita," Julie and Louisa said.

"All right," Nita said.

After breakfast, Mr. Patton and Georgie left the house, saddled up their horses, and rode off into the hills beyond Lake Vineyard.

When they got to one of their favorite campsites, Mr. Patton said, "Let's sit and talk for a while, Georgie." He grinned. "We won't be bothered by the womenfolk here."

Georgie grinned back.

After they had tied the horses to a small tree, they found a log and sat down together.

"I've told you many times, Georgie, that there's nothing too good for you, and I think it's time that you left the house to go to a regular school," Mr. Patton said. "If you stay at home much longer, only being tutored by your aunt

Nannie and me, then I think your intellectual growth will be stunted."

"Yes, Papa," Georgie said.

"I've enrolled you in the Classical School for Boys," Mr. Patton said. "It's located on South Euclid Avenue, in Pasadena. We've ridden by there many times, Georgie, so I'm sure you've seen it."

Georgie nodded. "Yes, sir," he said.

"I don't want you to be unhappy about this, Georgie," Mr. Patton said, "but I think it's the best thing for you."

"I'm not unhappy, Papa," Georgie said. "I'm looking forward to it."

School began the first Tuesday in September. Georgie was up early and ate breakfast by himself. He didn't want to see either his mother or Aunt Nannie, because ever since Mr. Patton had decided that Georgie would be continuing his education at the local grammar school, they had moped around the house, making it seem as though each day they were going to someone's funeral.

Mr. Patton drove Georgie to school himself in one of their best surreys. When they pulled up in front of the building, Mr. Patton shook hands with Georgie and said, "Son, when you step inside that front door, you will be starting a new life, apart from your family, but don't ever forget that our hearts and minds will never be separated, wherever you may be."

"Yes, sir, Papa," Georgie said.

As Georgie climbed out of the surey, he felt a lump forming in his throat. For a fleeting moment he thought about begging his father to take him back home, to the warmth and comfort he knew, but instead, he said, "I will make you proud of me, Papa, and I promise that I'll bring honor to the Patton name."

"That's all a father can ask, Georgie," Mr. Patton said.

Georgie turned and started toward the entrance of the school, where he saw two men

waiting for him. Behind him, he heard his father driving the surrey down the street, but he didn't look back. When Georgie reached the front steps, the two men came down to meet him, smiles on their faces and their hands extended.

"Good morning, Georgie. Welcome to the Classical School for Boys," the first man said. "I'm Dr. Stephen Cutter Clark, the principal, and we're delighted to have you with us."

"Thank you, sir," Georgie said.

The second man extended his hand and said, "I'm Mr. G. M. Clark, Dr. Clark's brother, and I'll be one of your teachers, Georgie. I want to extend my welcome to you too."

"Thank you, sir," Georgie repeated.

"Let's go inside now, Georgie," Dr. Cutter said. "My brother will show you to your class-room."

Mr. Patton had told Georgie all about the Clark brothers. Dr. Clark was a famous Latin scholar and historian, and Georgie was looking forward to learning as much as he could from him.

"We only have twenty-five students here, Georgie, and they're the sons of Southern California's most important families, so you will fit in well," Dr. Clark said. "Such a small student body means that we get to spend a lot of time with each of you, and you get to spend a lot of time with us."

"We'll know if you're studying, Georgie," Mr. Clark added. "There's no way you can fool us."

"Oh, I plan to study hard, sir, because I really want to learn everything I can," Georgie assured them.

"That's the right attitude," Dr. Clark said. They had stopped in front of a classroom. "Well, here we are. Your education at the Classical School for Boys begins."

Over the next year, Georgie tried very hard to excel in every subject he had, but he just couldn't seem to grasp mathematics, especially algebra and geometry.

"I try, Papa, I really try," Georgie told his father one evening after a particularly hard day. He hadn't understood the day's assignment and was instructed to show Mr. Patton a failing paper. "I just don't understand what Mr. Clark is trying to get me to do."

Instead of scolding Georgie, Mr. Patton sat with him at the kitchen table and patiently went over each problem. In the end, though, Georgie didn't think he understood it any more than he had when Mr. Clark had explained it.

"I'm just stupid, that's all," Georgie said angrily. "I'm just plain stupid, and I'll never amount to anything."

Mr. Patton took Georgie by the shoulders and looked him straight in the eyes. "You are not stupid, Georgie, and I don't ever want to hear you say that again," he said. "Not everyone is good in math, and you may never excel in this subject, but you'll just have to keep trying, and I don't want you even to think about giving up."

Georgie took a deep breath and let it out. "I won't give up, Papa, ever," he said. "I promise."

When Georgie got his first report card, most of his grades were in the fifties and sixties, with a few in the low seventies, but he got high marks for behavior, and his grades for history, both ancient and modern, were in the high nineties.

"Oh, Georgie! That's wonderful, my dear boy," Aunt Nannie said when she saw the report card. "I honestly didn't think you were remembering all of those books we read, but I was wrong, and this report card proves it."

"Will you read to me tonight, Aunt Nannie?" Georgie asked.

"Oh, yes, child, I most certainly will," she replied.

What had begun as a struggle for Georgie was now a challenge, and he had secretly vowed that he would be better than anyone else in the class. During the summer break, Georgie tried to reread every book he had been assigned for every class that first year, but he would often have to give up and ask Aunt Nannie if she would read them to him.

When school began that second year, Georgie felt a little more at ease. He had practiced reading and writing, but he still had problems.

"Dr. Clark! Would you ask Mr. Patton to reread that sentence?" another student would ask. "I'm quite sure I didn't understand what I just heard."

When the laughter subsided, Georgie would try again, despite Dr. Clark's telling him that he didn't have to. He often repeated his mistakes, his face turning bright red from anger and embarrassment, but he would continue to the end and then he would take his seat, his head still held high.

When Georgie wrote on the chalkboard, he would hear a student call, "Mr. Clark! Would you please ask Mr. Patton what language he's writing in? I simply don't recognize some of the letters he's using."

Once again, when the laughter had subsided, George would erase the blackboard, then take a piece of chalk and rewrite the sentence, trying to make sure that he formed his letters with care, but when laughter erupted behind him, he would know that he still hadn't succeeded.

Where Georgie excelled, though, was in his ability to memorize and quote word for word long passages from the Bible or the other books his father and Aunt Nannie had read to him. In history classes, especially, there was no laughter, only amazement, when Georgie would sometimes talk for over an hour about the topic at hand.

Eventually, the rest of the students were so amazed by his ability to memorize that they started to overlook the things he couldn't do.

Georgie really liked the Clarks' school. He only saw his struggles as a challenge. Nita was now attending Miss Anna Orton's Classical School for Girls in Pasadena, and they would often share stories and help each other solve some of their problems.

Georgie also began to spend more and more time in the school's library. It wasn't large, just a room at the back of the building, but it had what Georgie considered a wealth of books about military campaigns all through history. Georgie was fascinated by the ways wars have been waged over the centuries.

Encouragement and Creative Spelling

"Georgie?"

Georgie blinked, suddenly realizing that Dr. Clark was calling his name. He was not with Epaminondas, fighting battles in ancient Greece, but still at school. He noticed that there was very little light coming in through the one window on the west side.

"Yes, sir, Dr. Clark?" Georgie said. He pushed back his chair and stood. "I'm over here."

When Dr. Clark appeared, he said, "No one knew you were still here, Georgie. Your father is in my office, worried because you didn't return home when you were expected."

Georgie suddenly remembered that he was supposed to ride home with either Tom Bard or Charles Nordhoff, whoever left later, and when he had failed to show up, he was sure they both assumed he had gone with the other.

"I was reading about Epaminondas, sir," Georgie explained. "I guess it took me longer than I thought it would, and I forgot where I was."

"That can happen, Georgie," Dr. Clark said. "I myself forget where I am when I'm reading history."

"Do you really, sir?" Georgie said.

Dr. Clark nodded. "Quite!" he said. "Have you finished yet?"

Georgie shook his head. "Some of the words are still hard for me, sir, and I have to study them before I can go on to the next line," Georgie said, "but I don't mind because I want to learn all I can about famous military commanders."

"Yes, your father told me you wanted to make the army your life, Georgie, and I think . . ." Dr. Clark stopped. He chuckled. "Now, your father is probably beginning to wonder what has happened to *me*." He pinched his chin. "I have an idea. I still have some work to do here myself, so why don't I tell your father that I'll take you home. It's not that far out of the way, and I am always delighted when one of my students wants to spend this much time in the library."

"Oh, thank you, sir. I really would appreciate that," Georgie said. "I had just gotten to the exciting part of the story."

Dr. Clark left the library, and Georgie went back to the story of Epaminondas.

Later, Dr. Clark returned and said, "Well, I think we'd both better leave or our families will certainly think we've deserted them."

"Yes, sir," Georgie said. He closed the book and stood up. "I didn't finish, but I can do that tomorrow, if it's all right, sir."

"Of course, it is," Dr. Clark said. "Why don't you ask your father if I may take you home again tomorrow night, and that way he won't worry?"

"Yes, sir," Georgie said.

As they left the school in Dr. Clark's surrey, he said, "Tell me what you learned today, Georgie."

"I learned that no matter how long it may take, good always triumphs over evil, sir," Georgie said, "and that's what I see every time I read about military campaigns in history."

"I hope you also learned that sometimes it doesn't happen right away, though, and that from time to time, evil men get the better of good men," Dr. Clark said, "but when you're fighting for your country, when you're fighting for your civilization, not just for yourself and the spoils of war, you will be successful in the end."

Georgie nodded. "Yes, sir," he said.

"I'm curious about something, Georgie. Why do you like Epaminodas so much?" Dr. Clark asked. "Why not Themistocles or Cleon, or Alexander the Great or Caesar, or Constantine or Hannibal?"

"Themistocles was egotistical, although he probably had a right to be, and Cleon was a man of violent passions, but sometimes this seemed to cloud his thinking, so I don't think he was always successful. And when Alexander took his own life, his empire fell to pieces, and the others, well, sir, they just don't seem, in the end, that is, to match up with Epaminodas," Georgie said. "He was the greatest Greek who ever lived, I think. He was a good man, and he fought battles without personal ambition. He was a great patriot, and his battle strategies show true genius."

"He sounds just about perfect, Georgie," Dr. Clark said.

They had reached Lake Vineyard, and Dr.

Clark had stopped the surrey in front of the house.

"For the age in which he lived, I do think Epaminondas was the perfect man, sir," Georgie said. He stepped out of the surrey, then turned and shook hands with Dr. Clark. "Thank you for the ride home, sir, and for talking to me about history."

"Oh, it was my pleasure, Georgie, I can assure you," Dr. Clark said. "I'll see you tomorrow morning. Good night."

"Good night, sir," Georgie said.

Just as Georgie started up the steps, Dr. Clark said, "What do you really want to be, Georgie?"

Georgie stopped, turned around, and said, "I want to be just like Epaminodas, sir. For the age in which I live, I want to be the perfect man, too."

Over the next few months the Clarks encouraged Georgie to write down his thoughts about what he was reading, and even though it was a great struggle and at times neither of the Clarks could make out Georgie's creative spelling, he was able to show them the solid mind behind the learning disabilities he had to deal with every day.

"What you've written is both logical and patriotic, Georgie," Dr. Clark told him often. "You're a credit to your ancestors, son, and you have a great future ahead of you, I have no doubt."

When Georgie showed Nita an essay he had written about the siege warfare of the Normans, she said, "But Georgie, how could you have gotten such a good grade on this when you misspelled so many words?"

"What do you mean?" Georgie asked.

"Well, look at this," Nita said. "Here, you wrote 'a-t-a-c-k' and you should have written 'a-t-t-a-c-k.'"

"What difference does that make, Nita?" Georgie demanded, though not angrily, because he never got angry when Nita criticized him. "It sounds the same whether it has one 't' or two."

"Well, then, what about this?" Nita said, pointing to another word. "You wrote 'r-e-n-u-e-d' when you should have written 'r-e-n-e-w-e-d.'"

Georgie looked at the word. "Say it for me, Nita," he said.

Nita said the word.

"See? Why does it need that 'e-w'?" Georgie asked. "I understood you perfectly."

Nita shrugged. "Well, I wish I had gone to your school instead of mine," she said. "I never could have gotten by with that, Georgie."

"Dr. Clark is more interested in what I think than in how I spell, Nita," Georgie said. "He says that a person's character determines whether his or her life will be a success or a failure, and that being a good person—someone who thinks of others first—well, that's more important to me than knowing how to spell." He grinned.

"Anyway, Nita, anybody can spell things the right way. I think it takes a pretty smart person to be as creative in his spelling as I am!"

Beatrice Ayer

At the beginning of the summer of 1902, Georgie, just a few months short of his seventeenth birthday, had a growth spurt that added not only to his height but also to the length of his feet!

"Georgie! Where are those shoes you split open when you tried to put them on the other day?" Nita had opened his bedroom door without knocking, something only she could get away with. "I promised Mary Beth I'd show them to her. Do you mind?"

"No, I don't mind, Nita," Georgie said. He

went back to reading a book about William the Conqueror. "They're in my closet."

But out of the corner of one eye, Georgie watched as Nita and Mary Beth hurried over and pulled out the pair of shoes in question. They burst into laughter.

Georgie had a grin on his face too, but he didn't say anything because he didn't want to get into a conversation with Mary Beth. The only girl he really liked talking to was Nita.

"Oh, Georgie!" Mary Beth said. "I can't believe this really happened!"

Georgie grunted but he kept his eyes on the page he had been reading.

"I've just never heard of anything so funny in all of my life, Georgie," Mary Beth continued. "Don't you think it's funny?"

Reluctantly, Georgie laid down his book. "No, it's not funny, Mary Beth. It's kind of scary, actually," he said solemnly. "Now I hold my breath every time I put on my shoes, wondering if it's going to happen again."

120

Mary Beth was looking at him wide-eyed, but behind her, Georgie could see that Nita was trying hard not to laugh.

"Come on, Mary Beth," Nita finally managed to say. "You have to leave because we're going to Los Angeles to meet some visiting relatives."

Georgie stood up and followed Nita and Mary Beth downstairs. He wanted to stay in his room and finish another one of the books Dr. Clark had sent home with him for the summer, but he had promised his parents that he would go with them to meet the Ayer family, who were coming in from Boston in their private railway car.

For weeks Georgie's parents had talked about nothing but the upcoming visit of these distant relatives. Frederick Ayer, almost fifty years older than his wife, Ellen, had become enormously wealthy from the patent medicine business. They had three children, Beatrice, Frederick, Jr., and Mary Katherine. As hard as he tried, Georgie could only remember their last visit vaguely, more than ten years ago, but now they were coming again to spend the summer with the Pattons and the Bannings on Santa Catalina Island.

"How are they related to us, Mama?" Nita had asked last night at dinner.

"The Banning boys are brothers of Ellen Ayer," Mrs. Patton told her.

Just then, Aunt Nannie let out a sigh of disgust and wrinkled her nose, and all of a sudden Georgie remembered a vivid moment from the Ayers' last visit. They had all been seated around the dining table in their house, arguing about politics, when Ellen had made a grand entrance, much like the actresses in some of the stage plays that Georgie had seen in Los Angeles. Before Ellen sat down, she went around the table, hugging and kissing everyone. Ellen's fingers were covered with jeweled rings, Georgie remembered, and on her arms she wore gold bracelets for each year of her marriage to Mr. Ayer. She also wore a fresh rose in her hair. That night, though, she reached Aunt Nannie last. Instead of hugging her, she took her chin in her hand, raised Aunt Nannie's face, and asked, "Annie, my dear, what do you really think of life?" For the first time that Georgie could ever remember, Aunt Nannie had nothing to say.

As they headed into Los Angeles to meet the Ayers' train, Georgie said, "Well, at least maybe Frederick and I can do some things together on the island."

"I'm sure there will be time for that, Georgie," Mrs. Patton said, "but I don't really want you spending all of your time with Frederick. Since you and Beatrice are the same age, I thought it would be nice if you could introduce her to some of your friends."

"All right, Mama," Georgie said. He opened his book about William the Conqueror and didn't give Beatrice Ayer another thought.

The train from Boston was just pulling into the station when the Pattons arrived, but it took a while for the Ayers' private car to be unhooked from the rest of the train and shunted to a side track.

When the Ayers finally alighted, Georgie took one look at Beatrice and backed away in disgust. Her auburn hair was worn in a long braid that went all the way down to the hem of her long skirt. In her arms she was cradling a porcelain doll.

Georgie pulled Nita back from the group. "Beatrice is still a child, Nita," he whispered. "My friends will all laugh at me if I escort her around the island."

Nita took Georgie by the arm. "You're my brother, Georgie, and I love you dearly," she said, "so I'm telling you as your sister *and as a girl* that you shouldn't make a decision about Beatrice based on your first impression."

Georgie looked at Nita, raised his left eyebrow, and narrowed his eyes.

Nita squeezed his arm. "Trust me, Georgie," she whispered. "Now, let's go say hello to her."

Later that evening, Georgie found himself pacing his room, unable to concentrate on the book he had planned to finish that evening. He was surprised that he was still thinking about Beatrice. Nita had been right: His first impression had been wrong. When Nita practically thrust him in front of his distant cousin, she turned out to be pretty, intelligent, and full of spirit.

"I guess escorting Beatrice won't be so bad after all," Georgie managed to whisper to Nita as they headed toward the surreys that would take them back to Lake Vineyard. "Of course, there are still a lot of things I'm planning to do that only men can do," he added.

Nita smiled at him. "Of course, Georgie," she said. "We women understand that."

• • •

Two days later, the Pattons and the Ayers rode to San Pedro to catch a steamboat to Santa Catalina.

"It won't take us as long to get there this summer," Mr. Patton told everyone. "The time has been reduced to one and a half hours."

On the trip over, Georgie told Beatrice about the previous summer when he had learned to sail.

"I think it would be lovely if you showed me how it's done," Beatrice told him with a smile.

"All right," Georgie agreed.

"I hear you're an expert fisherman, too," Beatrice said.

"I am. And to prove it, I'll show you a picture of a forty-five-pound yellowtail I caught a couple of summers ago," Georgie said. "Papa had it framed, and it's hanging on the wall of my bedroom in our cottage."

"I can hardly wait to see it, Georgie," Beatrice said. She tilted her head and smiled at him. "I hope you'll teach me how to fish, too."

"It would be my pleasure, Beatrice," Georgie said. He was sure that he sounded like he had a frog in his throat.

"I've so been looking forward to our trip out here, but I was afraid that you wouldn't want to spend any time with a girl," Beatrice said, "so I was all prepared to entertain myself."

"Oh, no, I would never have let you do that," Georgie said. "When Mama and Papa first told me that you and your family would be spending the summer here, I immediately started thinking about all the things we could do."

Beatrice took Georgie's hand. "Oh, you are just the sweetest thing," she said.

Georgie gulped. What in the world was happening to him? he wondered.

As it turned out, the summer of 1902 was the most memorable one Georgie had ever spent on the island. From time to time he and

128

Frederick did things together, but Georgie surprised himself by mostly thinking about ways he could entertain Beatrice. He found joy in showing her all of the things that had made his previous summers on the island so enjoyable. He couldn't ever remember laughing so much, especially with a girl.

At the beginning of August, Mrs. Ayer, who had become friends with a couple of playwrights trying to start a summer theater program on the island, decided to take matters into her own hands and put on one-act plays that would star members of her family. The two playwrights agreed to help however they could.

As it turned out, every play that Mrs. Ayer chose had Georgie and Beatrice in the lead roles. Nobody complained, though, because not only was everyone in the cast having fun, they all thought that Georgie and Beatrice were the best actors in the family.

● ● ●

The Bannings gave a big party the night before the Pattons and the Ayers were to return to the mainland. Georgie had never had such a magical summer, he told Beatrice, and he wasn't looking forward to her leaving, but she had her studies and her social life in Boston and he still needed to complete his final year at the Classical School for Boys.

"May I write to you, Beatrice?" Georgie asked.

"Of course you may," Beatrice said. "I'll eagerly await your letters."

The Final Decision

At the end of the summer of 1902, Georgie was not only in love with Beatrice Ayer but had also decided that the time had come to make his dreams a reality and fulfill what he had always considered his destiny: to be an officer in the United States Army.

"I believe it is my obligation, as the heir to the Patton name, to carry on the tradition of becoming a great soldier," Georgie told his parents one evening.

"You have made a wise decision," Mr. Patton said.

"Oh, Georgie, I am so proud of you," Mrs. Patton said.

Mr. Patton looked at Mrs. Patton and said, "I think it's about time we stopped calling him 'Georgie' and started calling him 'George,'" he said.

George blushed. He had wanted to say the same thing, although he wasn't quite sure how to broach the subject. There was something else, though, that was even harder for him to talk about: where he would get his military training. All the Pattons had gone to the Virginia Military Institute, but George had decided that he wanted to seek admission to the United States Military Academy at West Point instead. He waited until later that evening, when his father was alone in his study, to talk to him.

"I know that VMI has trained three generations of Patton men to become soldiers, Papa," George told him, "but in my heart, I believe that the United States Military Academy at West Point is where I should go."

Mr. Patton nodded, but didn't say anything. Instead, he walked over to the fireplace, warmed his hands for a few minutes, then turned back around to face George.

"Acceptance to West Point can only occur by means of a presidential or a congressional appointment, George, and each candidate's academic record has to be outstanding," he said. "The Pattons have been at VMI since its founding, so your admission there is almost a certainty."

"I know, Papa," George said.

Mr. Patton turned back around and warmed his hands again. "But if West Point is what you have your heart set on, what you truly believe is the right direction for you," he said, "then I'll start contacting friends of ours who can help."

"Thank you, Papa," George said.

"I only ask this of you, George," Mr. Patton added. "If for some reason you're unable to gain admission to West Point, then I want you to attend VMI, even though your graduation from there won't guarantee you a commission in the army."

"I promise, Papa," George said.

Wanting to be true to his word, George started trying to write to Beatrice, but he couldn't seem to get the words he was thinking down on paper. His thoughts about military tactics had found their way to the written page, thanks to the help of the Clark brothers, but there was no way George was going to ask them to look over the letters he was writing to Beatrice. Instead, he did the best he could and decided he would have to trust that she was being honest when she said she eagerly awaited his letters.

George's only regret was that he hadn't prepared Beatrice for his poor spelling. But as she received his letters, Beatrice never once mentioned the misspelled words. Although she didn't write directly to George as much as he would have wished, she did quite often mention him in letters to other relatives, and they immediately informed him of what she had said. In a November letter, Beatrice asked an aunt to be sure and wish George a happy seventeenth birthday. For Christmas that year, Beatrice sent George a tiepin, and he sent her a thank-you note right away.

Mr. Patton wasted no time using his knowledge of how local politics worked to try to get George an appointment to West Point, but he reminded George from time to time that the process was a difficult one.

The first person Mr. Patton contacted was Senator Thomas R. Bard, the father of one of George's best friends. To help persuade Senator Bard that George deserved the appointment, Mr. Patton asked many of his friends to write Senator Bard in support of George. There were bank presidents, justices of the California Supreme Court, presidents of oil companies, many well-known lawyers, the naval aide to the governor of California, and the postmaster of Los Angeles. They all sent glowing letters, assuring Senator Bard that George Smith Patton, Jr., would have a distinguished career. For some reason, Senator Bard remained non-committal, as if all of the letters meant nothing. He only promised to make sure George received the same consideration as all of the other applicants.

"Why do you think he's behaving that way, George?" Mrs. Patton asked Mr. Patton one evening at dinner.

"He hates Rebels, that's why," Mr. Patton replied angrily. "He has no use for anyone who has their roots in proud Southern families."

At school, George worked even harder, staying until either Dr. Clark or his brother almost had to drag him out of the library. Still, he struggled with some of his subjects, often getting frustrated when, after studying many more hours than his other classmates, he still couldn't achieve their higher grades.

"It's a mystery to me, George," Dr. Clark would tell him, "but you really do keep getting better and better every day, so you must never give up."

"I won't ever give up, Dr. Clark, because a Patton would never do that," George assured him. "Anyway, I'm going to West Point, and that's all there is to that."

One evening, when George joined Mr. Patton in the study, he noticed that his father seemed more subdued than he had lately.

"What's wrong, Papa?" George asked.

"I've decided that you need another year of study before you take the West Point exam, George," Mr. Patton said, "but this may work to our advantage, because Senator Bard won't be appointing another student until next autumn."

George felt devastated, but he managed not to show it. "What do you think I should do, Papa?" he asked.

"I've written a letter to Mr. Francis C. Woodman, who's the headmaster of the Morristown School, in New Jersey," he said. "He has an excellent reputation for preparing students to enter West Point and all the Ivy League schools."

For the next few weeks, George found it difficult to concentrate because West Point now seemed so far away, but he managed to hide his feelings from everyone and eventually he was able to convince himself that it was only a momentary setback.

One day in early May, when George was sitting in the library with the window open, enjoying the breeze, Dr. Clark came in and said, "Mr. Woodman, the headmaster of the Morristown School, wants me to give you an examination, George, so I've scheduled it for tomorrow."

"All right," George said.

He didn't even bother to ask what the examination was for, but the next day, when he finished, his spirits were high because he thought that, with the exception of plane geometry, he had done very well.

Dr. Clark had the examination graded the next morning. "I am extremely proud of you, George. The results are very encouraging," he said. "I have no doubt that you scored high enough to enter West Point, if you get the appointment, but if you don't, you might think about one of the Ivy League schools."

Two months later, the Pattons received a letter from Mr. Woodman, telling them that he had taken the liberty of submitting George's test scores to Princeton University and that George had been granted admission to the class of 1907. For several days, George and everyone else in his family thought he would be leaving for New Jersey in September.

George had even begun to believe that his family wanted him to attend Princeton because someone had convinced them that he would bring dishonor to the Patton name at VMI, but then one morning, at breakfast, Mr. Patton said, "George, I've decided that the Virginia Military Institute is the only place to prepare you for West Point. You'll be leaving for Lexington in September."

"Thank you, Papa," George said.

Virginia Military Institute

The night before George left for VMI, he went for a walk around the Lake Vineyard estate with his uncle Andrew Glassell.

"I'm worried about something, Uncle Andrew, and I don't want to talk to Papa about it," George said.

"Well, George, I honestly can't imagine what that would be," Uncle Andrew said, "because I'm frankly envious of the close relationship you've always had with your father."

"Yes, we are very close, Uncle Andrew," George said, "but . . . well, it's just that . . . I'm afraid that I might turn out to be a . . . *coward*."

Uncle Andrew stopped and took George by the shoulders. "No Patton could ever be a coward, so you don't have a thing to worry about," he said. "It's not in your blood. It's not in your *heritage*."

"How do you know, Uncle Andrew?" George asked. "I've never really been in a fight before."

"Because you're a member of the American aristocracy, George, the *gentility*, even though nobody calls it that today," Uncle Andrew said, "and while that breeding might make you reluctant to engage in something so common as a fistfight, that same breeding allows you to face death on the field of battle with a smile on your lips."

As they continued their walk through the vineyard, George thought about the difference and realized that his uncle spoke the truth. At school, when some of the boys got angry and started fights, he instinctively shrank away from the crowd of other boys who seemed to want to join in, but when he was reading about major military campaigns throughout history, he dreamed of being on the field of battle, fighting for the glory of God and country.

As they started back toward the house, Uncle Andrew said, "George, there will soon be a great war that I think will engulf the entire world, and you need to prepare yourself for it, because I honestly have no doubt that you will play a major role in it."

Early the next morning, a hired coach arrived to take George, his parents, Nita, and Aunt Nannie into Los Angeles to catch the train to Virginia. The trip took them first to San Francisco, then to Salt Lake City, and finally to Lexington. It was an arduous journey, but George managed to keep everyone's spirits high. Inside, though, he was anxious. He knew it was his last chance to prepare himself for West Point, where he hoped to live up to the achievements of all the Patton men who had preceded him.

After several days of meetings with the officers and other staff at the Institute, the Pattons boarded a train that would take them back to Los Angeles, but Aunt Nannie had decided that she wanted to stay nearby. In case George needed anything, she would be there for him, she said, so she rented a house in town.

One of the first things that George had to do was get fitted for his uniforms. On the morning after his family left, he went to see the school tailor.

"Ah, Mr. Patton!" the tailor said. "I've been expecting you, sir."

George wasn't quite sure what to say.

144

"Actually, sir, we all have, in fact," the tailor continued. "The Pattons are a major part of the history of VMI, sir, and it's been too long since a Patton was here."

"Thank you," George managed to say.

When the tailor finished with his tape measure, he said, "I should have known, sir. You really didn't have to come for this fitting, because your uniform measurements are the same as your father's and grandfather's."

George felt overjoyed. He saw this as a sure sign that he belonged at VMI.

Even though George was now the lowest of the low—a first-year underclassman—he was surprised at how comfortable he felt at VMI. He was among the sons of graduates and other Southern gentlemen, where he knew he belonged. When classes started, he was even more surprised by how well he did, and it wasn't long until, out of the ninety students in his class, he was near the top in drawing, mathematics, Latin, history, and English. His behavior was worthy of praise too. Unlike many of his classmates, he received no demerits on his first report card.

As the days grew shorter and colder, some of the cadets began to grumble, especially those from states that hardly ever had much snow, but George found himself happier than he had ever been. His roots were there in Virginia, he knew, and he felt at home.

George used the moments when he was crossing from building to building to recall all of his family's advice about how to be a good soldier and a good scholar, but what he seemed to remember most was his father's advice about what to do on the nights before he was to march on guard duty.

"You should clean and shine your gun and brass until they're spotless, George," Mr.

Patton had said, "and if there is time left over, then you should study."

At VMI, George easily fell into his routine, but he was amazed at how often some of his classmates got into trouble.

"What's the secret, Patton?" Philip Masters whispered to him late one night after lights were out. "You seem to have all of the answers."

"You need to keep your mouth shut, Masters," George said. "You should never, ever talk back to the upperclassmen or to our instructors."

George heard Masters let out a sigh as his head flopped back on his pillow. "I'll never make it, Patton," he whispered. "I'll never make it."

"You can make it, Masters," George said, "if you just do what I do."

To George, it was all about character, and there were times when he thought most of his classmates didn't understand that. He liked them, and they were gentlemen to the core, but none of them seemed to have whatever it was that set the Pattons apart from everyone else militarily.

George's carriage was ramrod straight, and his uniform never had a wrinkle in it. His drill movements were perfect, and his equipment always seemed to be polished more brightly than any other cadet's.

After so many years of feeling stupid, George finally felt vindicated, now that he was accomplishing something. He was six feet tall and weighed 150 pounds, and he believed that he was the model soldier, but he wasn't alone in feeling that. So did everyone else at VMI—instructors, officers, and fellow cadets.

At the request of several of his classmates, George went out for the position of left tackle on the scrub football team and made it, but he never quite got the hang of the game.

"I think I'm the worst football player in the world," George admitted to a couple of his closest friends.

"Well, you really aren't very good," one of them told him.

George laughed. "I'm still glad I went out for the team, though," he said, "because I think I finally understand what people mean when they talk about VMI's fighting spirit."

At the beginning of December, George's grades in some subjects began to slip, and he started to worry that all of his early success at VMI was just luck and he would soon be struggling again. Although he was able to hide it, he was depressed for days. At first, he planned to ask for permission to visit his aunt in town, but then he decided that he was being tested by the ghosts of his VMI ancestors to see if he had the fortitude to achieve the goal he had set for himself: to go to West Point. He knew that what happened was up to him, and up to him only, and he immediately started studying even harder. It wasn't long until all of his grades improved and things were back to normal. Shortly afterward, George received a telegram from his father telling him that the entrance examination for West Point would be held in Los Angeles in mid-February.

With the blessings of everyone at VMI—and accompanied by Aunt Nannie—George boarded the train for Los Angeles at the beginning of February 1904 and studied for almost the entire six days of the trip. In his room at Lake Vineyard, George studied for another six days.

On the morning of February 15 Mr. Patton awakened George, sat with him while he dressed, and then the two went downstairs to breakfast.

George was so nervous, he let his ham and

eggs get cold, but he did manage to finish a biscuit with honey.

On the ride into Los Angeles, Mr. Patton said, "I don't want you to fear this test, George, because I think you have done all you can to prepare yourself for it."

"I've tried, Papa, I really have," George said, "and I will do the best I can."

"That's all anyone can ask of you, George," Mr. Patton said. "I know you're doing the right thing too, because if you stayed at VMI instead of taking your chances with West Point, then I think you would have a lifetime of regret."

George nodded. "Yes, sir," he said.

Four young men, including George, took the competitive West Point examination, given in a small room in Senator Bard's office suite in downtown Los Angeles. George was the last one to finish.

On the ride back to Lake Vineyard,

Mr. Patton said, "How did you feel about it?"

"I think I did very well, Papa," George told him, "but I guess we'll just have to wait to find out for sure."

The next morning, Mr. and Mrs. Patton and Nita drove George and Aunt Nannie into Los Angeles for the si x-day train trip to Virginia.

Back at VMI, George threw himself into every activity with a vengeance. He had promised himself that he wouldn't think about the examination. So when a telegram reached him on March 5, 1904, he was almost taken by surprise. It read:

SENATOR BARD HAS NOMINATED YOU FOR
WEST POINT!

It seemed to George that everyone at VMI was crowded into his room, congratulating him on the nomination.

"Thank you all so much," George told

them. "As my father told me many times, that which a man desires most strongly to do in this world, if he has really given it careful consideration, is generally what he is most fitted to do."

West Point

George arrived at West Point in June 1904, and right away he knew he belonged.

More than anything else, George wanted to do well, and he spent many hours studying, but once again he found himself struggling. Again, it was hard for him to understand how the other cadets could study less and get better grades than he did. He often got up before dawn to study, but still his final grades were below what was expected of him, so he was forced to repeat the first year.

For anyone else, this could have been

career-ending, but not for George S. Patton, Jr. In fact, he believed it was the best thing that could have happened to him, because he seemed to relax more and was able to make higher grades in every one of his classes, but he was also determined never to fail again, and he didn't. He played football so hard that he twice broke his arm. He also took up fencing and he quickly became the best swordsman in the class. Later, he even wrote the official fencing manual for the United States Army.

George was determined to look and act like a soldier, and he did this better than any of the other cadets. When the cadets were standing at attention, no one stood straighter than George. During his last year at West Point, he was named second in command of all the cadets. It was his job to read out the orders from the center of the parade ground.

George graduated from West Point in June 1909. He was twenty-three years old

and now a second lieutenant in the United States Cavalry. Mr. and Mrs. Patton, Nita, Aunt Nannie, and Beatrice attended the ceremony.

In September, George reported for his first duty assignment at Fort Sheridan, near Chicago, Illinois. He enjoyed his duties, but one thing was missing: Beatrice. They were married on May 26, 1910, and would eventually have three children, Beatrice, Ruth Ellen, and another George Smith Patton, Jr.

In December 1911, George transferred to Fort Myer, Virginia, just across the Potomac River from Washington, D.C.

In May 1912, George was selected to represent the United States in the Modern Pentathlon in the 1912 Olympic Games, to be held in Stockholm, Sweden. This meant he would compete in five sports at one time. He would have to run, swim, shoot, ride a horse, and fence. George finished fifth in the event. Before the shooting competition, he was actually leading, but his second shot appeared to miss the target. He told the judges that his second bullet had gone through the hole made by the first. They didn't believe him.

After the Olympics, George studied fencing and swordsmanship in France.

In September 1913, George and Beatrice moved to Fort Riley, Kansas, where George attended and graduated from the U.S. Army's Mounted Service School.

In September 1915, they moved to Fort Bliss, Texas, near El Paso. Six months after they arrived, Mexican raiders under Pancho Villa attacked the town of Columbus, New Mexico, killing eighteen Americans. The army was ordered to capture the Mexicans, even if they had to cross the border. This became known as the Mexican Border Campaign of 1916.

At the time, George was assigned to the Thirteenth Cavalry Regiment and he thought he would be going, but his name wasn't on the final list, so he went to General John J. Pershing and asked to accompany him. When Pershing wanted to know why he should take George with him, George told him that it was because he wanted to go more than anyone else did at Fort Bliss. General Pershing finally agreed to include him.

At first, the American troops met with no success, but at one farm house, where George had been sent to buy some corn, he had a hunch that the raiders were hiding on the premises. George, accompanied by ten soldiers from the Sixth Infantry Regiment, returned to the farmhouse in three automobiles. They surrounded it, killed General Julio Cárdenas, commander of Villa's personal bodyguard, and captured the other raiders. After this, Pershing referred to George as his own "Bandito." The incident made George's name a household word in the United States because it was the first time that automobiles instead of horses had been used in a battle.

Back at Fort Bliss, there was no time to celebrate, though, because all everyone wanted to talk about was the coming war in Europe.

Tanks!

The United States entered World War I on April 6, 1917, and soon afterward George, now commanding officer, Headquarters Staff, American Expeditionary Force, sailed for Europe. When he arrived, he learned that some soldiers were using a new invention called a tank—a machine with metal belts instead of wheels that allowed it to go through thick brush or climb over rocks. Right away, George wanted to know more about how they could be used to fight the enemy, so he asked to be assigned to the army's Tank Corps, and he reminded the general in charge that he was the only American ever to lead an attack in a motorized vehicle. He was referring to his participation in the capture of Pancho Villa's men in Mexico. Not only was George assigned to the Tank Corps, he was put in charge of it.

In September of 1918 George's Tank Corps participated in the St. Mihiel (France) offensive against German troops. Later that month, the corps took part in the Meuse-Argonne offensive. During the battle, George was wounded by machine gunfire when he tried to help some of the tanks that were mired in the mud. He was awarded a Purple Heart and a Distinguished Service Cross. He was also promoted to full colonel. While George was recuperating from his wounds, though, World War I ended on November 11, 1918, his thirty-third birthday. The United States and its Allies had won, but George was disappointed that there would be no more battles for him to fight.

In March 1919 George, now fully recovered, returned with his troops to the United States. While on duty at Camp Meade, Maryland, George became close friends with Lieutenant Colonel Dwight D. Eisenhower, who would play an enormous role in George's career in the future.

In 1920 George tried to get the United States Congress interested in providing more funding for an armored tank force for the army, but he wasn't very successful. Undeterred, George wrote several magazine and journal articles on how tanks could be used to fight battles. He also worked on improving the capabilities of the tanks. Eventually, though, he accepted the fact that in peacetime, the government wasn't interested in military innovation, so in order to advance his career, George transferred back to the cavalry, which was still using horses.

In 1923 George attended the army's Command and General Staff College, in Fort

Leavenworth, Kansas, where he graduated with honors. He was then assigned to staff duty in Hawaii.

In early 1932 George returned to duty at Fort Myer, Virginia, as the executive officer, Third Cavalry Regiment. Not too long after his arrival, Army Chief of Staff General Douglas MacArthur asked George to lead the charge against disgruntled veterans, known as the Bonus Army, who had marched on Washington, D.C., demanding money that they said the government had promised them for fighting in World War I.

In 1939 when Germany invaded Poland, starting World War II, George was finally able to convince Congress of the need for armored divisions. George was promoted to brigadier general and put in command of the armored brigade, but George didn't like what he saw in the new troops. He thought they looked too sloppy, so he ordered them to dress neatly, shine their shoes, and cut their hair. Once, during a huge practice battle in the South, all of the tanks ran out of gas, so George used his own money to buy gasoline at some of the local gas stations. When the other commanders told him this was against the rules, George said there were no rules in war! His tank brigade eventually became the United States Second Armored Division, and George was promoted to major general.

In July 1940 George was appointed commanding officer, Second Armored Brigade of the Second Armored Division, Fort Benning, Georgia. Slowly but surely, he was finally realizing his dream of having the best tank-fighting force in the world. It seemed to George that there was no way that the United States could keep from being drawn into World War II, and George looked forward to returning to battle, something he had planned for all of his life.

World War II

A few months after the Japanese attacked the United States Naval Base at Pearl Harbor, Hawaii, on December 7, 1941, George established the Desert Training Center for tanks and other mechanized vehicles at Indio, California. He knew that sooner or later, the United States would be involved in desert battles. By August, George was on a ship, headed for England, where he would help plan for the United States' invasion of North Africa.

On November 8 George commanded the first United States Armored Corps of the U.S.

Army, which landed on the coast of Morocco in Operation Torch. George and his staff were aboard the heavy cruiser USS *Augusta*, which came under fire from the Vichy French battleship *Jean Bart* when it entered Casablanca harbor, but the American troops finally managed to land and start their long trek across North Africa to fight the German troops.

Their first battle was a disaster, though. In early March of 1943 the German Afrika Corps defeated the Americans at the Battle of the Kasserine Pass in Tunisia. Afterward, George was put in command of the United States Second Corps in hopes of revitalizing it so there would be no further battlefield losses. Although George was tough in his training, he was considered fair. His troops also liked and respected him. He insisted on strict discipline and it paid off, because by the end of the month, the United States forces were victorious at the Battle of El Guettar and had begun a counteroffensive that was pushing the Germans back toward the east. At the same time, the British Eighth Army, under the command of General Bernard Law Montgomery, was in Egypt and had begun pushing the Germans back to the west. The effect of all of this was to squeeze the Germans out of North Africa.

Because of his accomplishments in North Africa, George was given command of the United States Seventh Army to prepare it for the invasion of the Italian island of Sicily in July of 1943. According to the plans, George and his troops would invade the western part of the island, and General Montgomery and his troops would invade the eastern part, but George had an intense rivalry with Montgomery, so he and his men quickly pushed through western Sicily, liberated the city of Palermo, and then headed to the eastern part of the island, where they reached the city of Messina ahead of the British.

In early August 1943 something seemed to

happen to George. His personality began to change. Before the invasion of Sicily, George made a speech to his troops telling them to show the enemy no mercy. He said that the Germans and the Italians were responsible for the deaths of thousands of American soldiers and should be killed. Some people believed that speech caused what came to be know as the Biscari (Sicily) Massacre, in which American troops shot almost eighty defenseless German and Italian prisoners of war. The incident almost put an end to George's military career. Later that month, when George was visiting troops in a hospital, he slapped Privates Paul G. Bennett and Charles H. Kuhl and called them cowards for shirking their military duties because of imagined injuries. Actually, both soldiers were suffering from battle fatigue. George was immediately ordered by his superior officers to stay out of public view and to apologize to the soldiers. When the news of this incident reached the United States, there were demands that George either resign or be fired. In the end, George was only relieved of his command of the Seventh Army before it invaded mainland Italy. In January 1944 he was transferred to England.

In the period leading up to the Normandy invasion, on June 6, 1944, George played a large role in what was an Allied campaign to make the Germans thinks that the Allies would invade France by way of Calais. The deception worked.

Following the Normandy invasion, George was given command of the United States Third Army. During what was known as Operation Cobra, his troops took the city of Cherbourg and then moved south and east to help trap several hundred thousand German troops near the town of Falaise. George actually used the German's own tactics of moving at lightning speed. He and his troops covered six hundred miles in just two weeks. George's forces freed

most of northern France and encircled Paris, but it was decided to let French troops under French Marshal Philippe de Hauteclocque liberate the city itself.

On August 31, 1944, George's troops ran out of gasoline near the Meuse River, just outside the French city of Metz. The time it took to get resupplied was just long enough to allow the Germans to fortify Metz, but three months later, after heavy fighting and many casualties, Metz finally fell to the Americans.

In late 1944 the German army began an offensive across the Netherlands, Luxembourg, and northeastern France. This was called the Battle of the Bulge. On December 16 over a quarter million German soldiers attacked the Allied lines and made massive headway toward the Meuse River during one of the worst winters in Europe in years. Almost immediately, George turned his Third Army north to help relieve the 101st Airborne Division, which was trapped in Bastogne. Afterward, everyone agreed that no other general but George S. Patton, Jr., could have accomplished such a feat. By February 1945 the Germans were once again in full retreat. George and his troops moved into the Saar River basin of Germany. His plans were to take Prague, Czechoslovakia, but he was ordered to halt his offensive. A decision had been made in Washington, D.C., that would allow the Soviet Union to conquer most of Eastern Europe instead.

On May 8, 1945, World War II in Europe ended, but the war in the Pacific was still raging.

The Last Months

With the war over in Europe, George requested a combat command in the Pacific, but the army refused to give it to him, and he was very disappointed.

Back in the United States, though, George rode in several military parades, cheered by thousands of Americans who wanted to see the hero they had read so much about during the war. George also spent a month with his family, whom he hadn't seen in almost three years.

When George returned to Europe, he was

appointed military governor of Bavaria, one of Germany's southern states, but he soon began suffering from bouts of depression because he was sure he would never fight in another war. He also began having more trouble with his superior officers. Once again there was an outcry when he said that the Nazis were like American politicians who lost elections. George was soon relieved of his Third Army command and transferred to the Fifteenth Army, where his only duty would be to write a history of the war. Many of George's friends believed that all of the head injuries that he had suffered during his life, from both war- and horse-related accidents, had in some way damaged part of his brain.

On December 9 George and his chief of staff, Hobart Gay, were in George's limousine, on their way to hunt pheasant near Mannheim, when they collided with an army truck. George was sent hurtling through the air. The accident paralyzed him from the neck down. No one else was hurt. George was taken to a hospital in Heidelberg, where he died twelve days later, his beloved Beatrice at his side.

George's early learning disability, which, late in his life, was diagnosed as dyslexia, is usually characterized by reading, writing, and spelling reversals, but that only scratches the surface of the problem. In very severe cases, it also affects a person's ability to concentrate and causes sharp mood swings, obsessiveness, impulsiveness, compulsiveness, and feelings of stupidity. There is also a tendency to boast. People who are dyslexic are quite frequently motivated by an overwhelming desire to prove that they are better than everyone else, but they are never satisfied with their accomplishments, and they are always pushing themselves to achieve more. This is an accurate description of George Smith Patton, Jr.—a genius in the art of war and one of America's greatest soldiers.

For More Information

BOOKS

Blumenson, Martin. *Patton: The Man behind the Legend, 1885–1945*. New York: William Morrow and Company, Inc., 1985.

Blumenson, Martin, ed. *The Patton Papers: 1885–1940*, Boston: Houghton Mifflin Company, 1974.

Blumenson, Martin, ed. *The Patton Papers: 1940–1945*. Boston: Houghton Mifflin Company, 1974.

D'Este, Carlo. *Patton: A Genius for War*. New York: HarperCollins Publishers, 1995.

Devaney, John. *"Blood and Guts": The True Story of General George S. Patton, USA*. New York: Julian Messner, 1982.

178

Farago, Ladislas. *Patton: Ordeal and Triumph*. New York: Ivan Obolensky, Inc., 1963.

Hirshson, Stanley P. *General Patton: A Soldier's Life*. New York: HarperCollins, 2002.

Lande, D. A. *I Was with Patton: First-Person Accounts of WW II in George S. Patton's Command*. Saint Paul, MN: MBI Publishing Company, 2002.

Patton, General George S. *War as I Knew It*. Boston: Houghton Mifflin Company, 1990.

Patton, Robert H. *The Pattons: A Personal History of an American Family*. New York: Crown Publishers, Inc., 1994.

Rice, Earle, Jr. *Strategic Battles in Europe*. San Diego: Lucent Books, Inc., 1999.

Smith, David Andrew. *George S. Patton: A Biography*. Westport, CT: Greenwood Press, 2003.

WEBSITES

http://www.generalpatton.org
http://www.generalpatton.com
http://www.pattonhq.com
http://www.desertusa.com/mag99/feb/stories/patton.
  html

180

★★★ **Childhood of Famous Americans** ★★★

One of the most popular series ever published for young Americans, these classics have been praised alike by parents, teachers, and librarians. With these lively, inspiring, fictionalized biographies—easily read by children of eight and up—today's youngster is swept right into history.

ABIGAIL ADAMS ★ JOHN ADAMS ★ LOUISA MAY ALCOTT ★ SUSAN B. ANTHONY ★ NEIL ARMSTRONG ★ ARTHUR ASHE ★ CRISPUS ATTUCKS ★ CLARA BARTON ★ ELIZABETH BLACKWELL ★ DANIEL BOONE ★ BUFFALO BILL ★ RAY CHARLES ★ ROBERTO CLEMENTE ★ CRAZY HORSE ★ DAVY CROCKETT ★ JOE DIMAGGIO ★ WALT DISNEY ★ AMELIA EARHART ★ DALE EARNHARDT ★ THOMAS EDISON ★ ALBERT EINSTEIN ★ HENRY FORD ★ BEN FRANKLIN ★ LOU GEHRIG ★ GERONIMO ★ ALTHEA GIBSON ★ JOHN GLENN ★ JIM HENSON ★ HARRY HOUDINI ★ LANGSTON HUGHES ★ ANDREW JACKSON ★ MAHALIA JACKSON ★ TOM JEFFERSON ★ HELEN KELLER ★ JOHN FITZGERALD KENNEDY ★ MARTIN LUTHER KING, JR. ★ ROBERT E. LEE ★ MERIWETHER LEWIS ★ ABRAHAM LINCOLN ★ MARY TODD LINCOLN ★ THURGOOD MARSHALL ★ JOHN MUIR ★ ANNIE OAKLEY ★ JACQUELINE KENNEDY ONASSIS ★ ROSA PARKS ★ GEORGE S. PATTON ★ MOLLY PITCHER ★ POCAHONTAS ★ RONALD REAGAN ★ CHRISTOPHER REEVE ★ PAUL REVERE ★ JACKIE ROBINSON ★ KNUTE ROCKNE ★ MR. ROGERS ★ ELEANOR ROOSEVELT ★ FRANKLIN DELANO ROOSEVELT ★ TEDDY ROOSEVELT ★ BETSY ROSS ★ WILMA RUDOLPH ★ BABE RUTH ★ SACAGAWEA ★ SITTING BULL ★ DR. SEUSS ★ JIM THORPE ★ HARRY S. TRUMAN ★ SOJOURNER TRUTH ★ HARRIET TUBMAN ★ MARK TWAIN ★ GEORGE WASHINGTON ★ MARTHA WASHINGTON ★ LAURA INGALLS WILDER ★ WILBUR AND ORVILLE WRIGHT

★★★ **Collect them all!** ★★★